THE BABY-SITTERS CLUB

Kristy's Mystery Admirer
Ann M. Martin

AN
APPLE
PAPERBACK

SCHOLASTIC INC.
New York Toronto London Auckland Sydney

Cover art by Hodges Soileau

ISBN 0-590-43567-1

12 11 10 9 8 7 6 5 4 3 2 1   0 1 2 3 4 5/9

Printed in the U.S.A.   40

First Scholastic printing, October 1990

For Jennifer and John

CHAPTER 1

"Concentate, concentrate," I said softly. Then I raised my voice. "Keep your eye on the ball!" I yelled.

I must have startled Jackie Rodowsky because he swung way too low and missed an easy pitch.

"Strike two!" shouted the umpire.

"Darn," I muttered. I went back to murmuring, "Concentrate, *con*centrate."

It was almost the end of another game between the Krushers and the Bashers. Who are the Krushers and the Bashers? They're softball teams here in Stoneybrook, Connecticut. I am the coach of the Krushers. Bart Taylor is the coach of the Bashers.

I have a crush on Bart.

Anyway, for the first time in the history of softball games between my Krushers and Bart's Bashers, it looked like the Krushers had a chance to win. See, the Krushers are not

1

your average softball team. The players are all kids who are too young or too scared to try out for T-ball or Little League. In other words, as you might have guessed, they aren't great players. (Well, most of them aren't.) One kid ducks every time a ball comes toward him. Most of the kids are not good hitters. We even have one player who's only *two and a half years old.* We let her use a special ball and bat so she doesn't get hurt, and we have to tell her everything to do. But you know what? She's a pretty good hitter for her age.

Bart's Bashers, on the other hand, are an older, tougher group of kids. (I don't know why they don't just join Little League. Maybe they like having Bart as their coach. I could certainly understand that.) The thing is, the Bashers have always beaten the Krushers easily.

Until now.

Now the score was tied, the Krushers had been playing *very* well, the bases were loaded, and it was the bottom of the ninth — with two outs. The only problem was that the Krushers were up, and our batter was Jackie Rodowsky, the walking disaster. Poor Jackie. I love him to bits, but he *is* a walking disaster. He's accident-prone, he has bad luck, and he's not too coordinated.

The pitcher looked nervous, though. After all, the game was tied, and the Bashers had never been beaten by the Krushers.

Still, this was the walking disaster at bat. "Come on, come on," I muttered, and gave Jackie the thumbs-up sign.

The pitcher threw the ball, Jackie swung his bat, and — he hit a home run! Four more runs.

"We won! We won!" the Krushers screamed.

I screamed right along with them, even though I knew the Bashers had been playing under handicaps. Their best hitter had the chicken pox, their usual pitcher was out of town for the weekend, and two good players had been benched for fighting (with each other).

Still, the Krushers were victorious, and our cheerleaders went wild. "We won! We won! We won!" they couldn't stop yelling. Then they remembered their softball manners and shouted, "Two, four, six, eight! Who do we appreciate? The Bashers! The Bashers! Yea!"

I had a feeling this was the first time our cheerleaders actually meant what they were saying.

Our cheerleaders, by the way, are Vanessa Pike and Haley Braddock, who are nine, and Charlotte Johanssen, who's eight. Haley's brother, Matt, is a Krusher. He's profoundly deaf, but he's one of our best players. We communicate with him using sign language. Several of Vanessa's brothers and sisters (she has *seven*) are on the team, including her littlest sister, Claire, who's five and sometimes throws tantrums, shouting, "Nofe-air! Nofe-air! Nofe-air!" when she thinks she's been wronged.

Anyway, I waited until all of my Krushers had been picked up by moms or dads or sitters or older brothers and sisters, and were heading home joyously, amid surprised and excited cries of "We *beat* the *Bashers!* Honest." And, "We finally won a game!"

Then I looked across the schoolyard to where my big brother Charlie was waiting to drive me and my little brothers and sister home. (Charlie is seventeen, can drive, and has this awful old secondhand car. At least it runs.)

Who am I? I'm Kristy Thomas. I'm thirteen and I'm an eighth-grader at Stoneybrook Middle School (SMS). I have three brothers, a stepbrother and stepsister, and an adopted sister. David Michael, my seven-year-old brother, and Karen and Andrew, my stepsister and stepbrother, who are seven and four, are Krushers. Charlie was going to drop Karen and Andrew off at their mother's house and then take David Michael and me home. This was nice of him. We could have walked, but we had an awful lot of equipment.

Charlie and I were just loading the last of it into the back of his car, when a voice said, "Can I walk you home?"

I whirled around. It was Bart.

My heart flip-flopped. It actually felt like it turned over inside my chest. I tried to breathe slowly.

"Charlie?" I asked. "Is that okay with you? You can leave the stuff in the car and I'll help you unload it as soon as I get home."

"No problem," replied Charlie. (He is so good-natured.)

"Okay, see you later, David Michael. Karen and Andrew, I'll see you Friday afternoon." (Karen and Andrew only live with their dad and my mom and the rest of our family every other weekend. Oh, and for two weeks during the summer. The rest of the time they live with their mother and stepfather.)

" 'Bye!" called David Michael, Karen, and Andrew, who were still practically hysterical over beating the Bashers.

Charlie drove off in his rattly car, and I looked at Bart. I wasn't sure what to say. Of course, I was ecstatic that we'd beaten his team. On the other hand, we'd *beat*en his *team*. Bart couldn't be feeling too great.

But — "Congratulations," said Bart sincerely. "Your kids sure have guts. They played really well today."

"Thanks," I replied. I was pleased. Really I was. But all Bart and I ever talked about was softball or our teams.

We walked a little way in silence. I couldn't think of a thing to say. At last Bart said, "Guess what happened in the locker room at school today?" (Bart does not go to SMS. He goes to Stoneybrook Day School, a private school.)

"What?" I asked, shuddering. Did I really want to know what went on in a boys' locker room?

"This guy," Bart began, "got a little crazy after gym class, and he was clowning around, swinging from the pipes on the ceiling. All of a sudden, this pipe breaks, he falls down onto the benches, and the sprinkler system goes off! Everybody got soaked."

I laughed. "What happened to the kid? Was he hurt?"

"Him? Hurt? Nah. His nickname is Ox. Nothing could hurt him."

"Once," I said, "we were playing field hockey and this girl who is completely un-

6

coordinated took a whack at the ball and it hit the teacher on the head!"

It was Bart's turn to laugh. Then he said, "Somehow I can't picture you in a field hockey kilt."

"They're not so bad," I replied. "The bloomers have changed. The uniforms are much more up-to-date now. . . . I do wish we could just wear jeans and T-shirts, though. Practically the only time I wear a skirt is when we play field hockey."

"You should wear skirts more often," said Bart.

"How come?" I asked.

Bart shrugged. Then he blushed. "I bet you'd look pretty, that's all."

"I'm not pretty in my Krushers outfit?" I asked. I was just teasing, but Bart blushed even redder. "Come on," I said. "Don't worry about it. I'm just giving you a hard time. So how's school?"

"Fine. The same old stuff."

"Yeah. For me, too."

"How's the Baby-sitters Club?"

"Great!" (My friends and I have a club that is really a business. We baby-sit for the families in our neighborhoods. I'll tell you more about it later.)

"And how are your friends?"

"What is this? A talk show?" I said, laughing.

Bart grinned. "I don't know. I mean, no. I just want to hear about your life . . . instead of softball."

I looked at Bart seriously. "Well, let's see. Mallory's really happy because she's going out with a guy for the first time. Claudia's doing better in school. But I'm a little worried about Stacey."

"Stacey," repeated Bart. "She's the one with diabetes, right?"

I nodded. "She's never really *sick*. She just doesn't seem *well* sometimes, if you know what I mean."

Bart nodded.

"How about you?" I asked. "How's everything?"

"Not bad. Kyle gets on my nerves, but I can handle him." (Kyle is Bart's little brother.) "My parents bug me, though. They hate it when my band practices in the basement."

"You have a *band?*" I said in amazement.

"Yup."

"What do you play?"

"Guitar. Electric, acoustic, any kind."

"I didn't know that. So have you had any . . . what are they called?"

"Gigs," supplied Bart. "Yeah, a couple. We

8

could get a lot more, though, if we could find a place to practice. *No* one wants us in their basement."

"What about a garage?"

"The neighbors complain."

"Oh."

Bart and I talked about his band and music and school until, before I knew it, we had reached my house.

Emily, my adopted sister, was sitting on the front steps with Nannie, my grandmother. She came flying out to meet me and gave me a tight hug around the knees.

"Hi, Emily," I said, picking her up. Then I called, "Hi, Nannie!"

Nannie waved to me.

"Well," said Bart, "I better get going. I told Mom I'd come home right after the game. But, um, I'll see you soon, okay?"

"Next game," I said.

"Maybe before that," Bart replied, and he walked off, whistling. I stared after him.

CHAPTER 2

"Hello, Emily-Boo," I said to my little sister. I carried her back to Nannie.

"I heard about the game today," said Nannie immediately. "David Michael was so excited, he could hardly stand it."

"Yeah, the Krushers played pretty well today." I turned to Emily. "Maybe someday you'll be a Krusher, too. Do you want to play softball?"

"Yes," replied Emily. (I knew she hadn't understood the question.)

Emily and Nannie and I went inside. Our house is sort of big. Actually, it's a mansion. My stepfather, Watson, is a millionaire. But thank goodness for the big house. When Mom married Watson we moved from our tiny house into his and needed room not just for Watson, my mother, my three brothers, and me, but for Karen and Andrew, and now Emily and Nannie. (Nannie is Mom's mother, my special grandmother who doesn't act like a grandmother at all. She goes bowling, wears pants, and has tons of friends.)

Anyway, Nannie began making dinner, so I watched Emily. When the phone rang, I shouted, "I'll get it!"

I picked up the phone in the den. "Hello?"

"Hi, it's me, Shannon."

"Hi!" Shannon lives across the street and she's the first friend I made when I moved into this ritzy neighborhood. (Well, we became friends after we stopped hating each other.) We don't see each other much, though, since she goes to Bart's school. She is a member of the Baby-sitters Club (BSC), but she doesn't come to meetings. (More about that later.)

"How'd the game go?" Shannon wanted to know.

I told her every last detail, and she was almost as excited as I was.

"Maybe I'll come to the next game," she said.

When we got off the phone, I felt happy — and lucky. I have an awfully nice group of friends in the BSC.

Emily came into the den then to watch *Sesame Street*. (She can't tell time, but somehow she always knows when the show is on.) I let Bert and Ernie and Big Bird and Cookie Monster fade into the background as I thought about my friends.

My best friend is Mary Anne Spier, the secretary of the club. (I am the president.) I used to live next door to her until Mom married Watson. Before I moved to Watson's, Mary Anne and I had grown up together. I lived with my mom and my brothers and my father — until he moved out. But Mary Anne lived with just her father, since her mother died when Mary Anne was really little.

Mr. Spier was very strict, raising Mary Anne on his own. He made up all these rules for her, but as Mary Anne has grown up, he's relaxed a lot. Maybe because her father was so strict, or maybe just because it's her nature, Mary Anne is shy and sensitive and cries easily. (She's just the opposite of me. I'm outgoing and have a big mouth, and it takes a lot to make me cry.) Mary Anne is also romantic and, although she's shy, she's the only one of us to have a steady boyfriend. His name is Logan Bruno, and he's funny and understanding, but I think he and Mary Anne have been having some problems lately.

Believe it or not, Mary Anne and I sort of look alike. We're both short (I'm the shortest in my class), and we both have brown hair and brown eyes. Mary Anne used to dress like a baby, since she had to do whatever her father said, but now that he's loosened up, Mary Anne's clothes have changed from little-girl to, well, not exactly sophisticated, but maybe almost trendy.

In the last few months Mary Anne has gone through some BIG changes, which I'll fill you in on, but first I have to tell you about Dawn Schafer. Dawn is what we call the club's alternate officer, and she is Mary Anne's other best friend. Dawn, her younger brother, Jeff, and her mom moved to Stoneybrook last year when we were in the middle of seventh grade. They moved because her parents had gotten a divorce, and Mrs. Schafer wanted to come back to the town where she'd been raised. This was fine for her, but not so easy for Dawn and Jeff, who had grown up in California. Dawn misses California but likes Stoneybrook okay. With Jeff, the story was different. He never adjusted to his new home, so after several months he moved back to California to live with his father. Dawn misses that half of her family terribly and visits them as often as she can. However, she now has a new father and a stepsister. And guess who her stepsister is — Mary Anne!

It turned out that Mary Anne's dad and Dawn's mom had been high-school sweethearts, only they'd gone their separate ways after they graduated. Then Mrs. Schafer moved back to Stoneybrook, she and Mr. Spier began seeing each other again, and after a long time, they got married! So now Dawn has a stepfather, Mary Anne has a stepmother, and it's one big, *usually* happy family. They all (including Tigger, Mary Anne's kitten) live in the colonial farmhouse that Dawn's mom bought when the Schafers moved to Connecticut.

Here are a few more things about Dawn. She's an individualist who stands up for what she believes in, even if no one else believes in it. She's organized (thank goodness, because her mom is exactly the opposite). She and her mom (and Jeff and her dad) *love* health food and don't eat meat. Dawn is gorgeous. She has LONG silky blonde hair. Honest, it's so blonde it's nearly white. She has sparkling blue eyes and she dresses like the individual she is. She wears what she wants to wear. My other friends and I think of it as "California casual." Dawn has *two* holes pierced in each ear. (Mary Anne and I will *never* get our ears pierced.)

The vice-president of the club is Claudia Kishi. When Mary Anne and I were still in our old neighborhood on Bradford Court, we lived across the street from Claudia. So she grew up with us, too. Claudia lives with her parents and her older sister, Janine, who is a genius. It's true. Janine is only in high school, but she gets to take courses at the local college. This is a tragedy where Claudia is concerned. See, the thing about Claud is that she's smart, but she doesn't *apply* herself, as her teachers are always pointing out. Claud would much rather read a good Nancy Drew book (she's hooked) or work on her art. Usually her art takes priority. (That means that it's more important.) And no wonder. Claudia is a fantastic artist. Her work is incredibly distant. (That's a word my friends and I made up to mean *super*cool.) Claud can sculpt, paint, draw, make collages, you name it. She even makes her own jewelry.

That's another thing. Claudia's clothes. She's a real fashion plate. Talk about distant. Her clothes are *so* distant. Claudia is the most interesting dresser I know. She is always wearing things like Day-Glo high-top sneakers, cut-up jeans, off-the-shoulder sweat shirts (sometimes torn), and friendship bracelets. (Her best friend is Stacey McGill, the club treasurer, and Claud braided friendship bracelets for both of them.)

Claud is exotic-looking. She's Asian and has

long black hair that she fixes a million ways, almond-shaped eyes, and a complexion I would die for. How come I get pimples sometimes and Claud *never* does? Especially since she's addicted to junk food. She hides it all over her room. (Her parents, naturally, don't approve of this.) Also, she has two holes pierced in one ear and one hole in the other.

As I mentioned, the BSC treasurer is Stacey McGill. Two things about Stacey: 1. She is *the* most distant of all of us. 2. She has had the most problems of all of us (in my opinion).

Stacey originally came from New York City. That's where she grew up, and I think that's why she's so sophisticated. Stacey's clothes are at least as distant as Claudia's, and she gets to have her hair permed and stuff. She has pierced ears, of course, and she is slightly boy-crazy. *But*, her life has not been easy. First, Stacey's father's company transferred him to Stamford, Connecticut, which is not far from Stoneybrook, so Stacey had to leave New York and her friends at the beginning of seventh grade. Then, the McGills had only been living here for about a year when Stacey's father was transferred *back* to New York. And not long afterward, the McGills decided to get a divorce. Not only that, Mrs. McGill planned to return to Stoneybrook, while Mr. McGill planned to stay in New York with his job. Who was Stacey going to live with? How would she make the decision? It wasn't easy at all, but finally Stacey returned to Stoneybrook and the BSC. Of course, us club members, especially Claudia, were thrilled, but Stacey still feels guilty about leaving her father. She visits New York a lot.

To top things off, as I mentioned before, Stacey has diabetes — a severe form of the disease. What that means is that something in her body called insulin can go out of whack if Stacey doesn't stick to a strict no-sweets, calorie-counting diet, give herself injections of insulin (yuck), and monitor her blood. I know this sounds disgusting, but think how Stacey feels. And I have to admit that she hasn't been looking good lately. There's talk of her going to see her special doctor in New York again.

The last two members of the Baby-sitters Club are younger than the rest of us. They're in sixth grade at SMS, and we're in eighth grade. Their names are Mallory Pike and Jessica Ramsey, but they mostly go by Mal and Jessi. (Mallory, by the way, is someone our club used to sit *for*.) Anyway, Mal and Jessi are best friends, and I can see why. They have a lot in common, although they certainly have their differences, too. First of all, they're both the oldest in their families, except that Mallory has *seven* younger brothers and sisters (she's Claire and Vanessa Pike's big sister), and Jessi has just one younger sister and a baby brother. Becca is eight,and Squirt (whose real name is John Philip Ramsey, Jr.) is a toddler. Both Mal and Jessi are at that awful age (eleven) when they want to be more grown-up than their parents will let them be. They *were* allowed to get their ears pierced recently, but Mal has to wear glasses and braces, so she doesn't feel particularly pretty, and both girls feel that their parents treat them like babies sometimes. Plus, Jessi's mother just got a job, so with both Mr. and Mrs. Ramsey working, Jessi's Aunt Cecelia moved in. Sometimes Jessi feels like Aunt Cecelia is *her* baby-sitter. A few more similarities: Mal and Jessi both like to read, especially horse stories, and to write. (Well, Mal likes writing more than Jessi does, but she *did* convince Jessi to keep a journal, which Jessi has been doing faithfully.)

Now for the differences. Mal, the great writer, would like to be an author and illustrator of children's books one day, while Jessi thinks she'd like to be a professional dancer. She's been taking ballet classes for years, dances *en pointe* (that means *on toe*), and has even had leading roles in several ballets, dancing in front of big audiences. She takes lessons a couple of times a week at a special school in Stamford, Connecticut. She had to *audition* just to be able to take lessons there.

Furthermore, Jessi and Mal couldn't look less alike if they tried. Jessi is black and Mal is white. Jessi has the long, graceful legs of a dancer, is thin, and has these huge, dark eyes with lashes that I'd like to have as much as I'd like Claudia's complexion. Mal, on the other hand, has unruly red hair, and (as I mentioned before) wears glasses and braces, so she's not too pleased with her appearance right now. Also, she has freckles, which she can't stand.

Let's see, I might as well finish telling you about me, as long as I'm on the subject of the members of the Baby-sitters Club. I am active, always on the go and coming up with new ideas. (Some people think I'm bossy.) Can you believe it? I'm the only club member who *still* doesn't wear a bra because I don't need one. I don't care too much about clothes, though, anyway. I am not trendy and distant like some of my friends. I'm more of a slob. Almost every day I wear jeans, running shoes, a turtleneck, and a sweater. Those clothes are *comfortable*.

I miss my father. He never calls or writes anymore. I wish he were more like Dawn's father or like Watson. They both make efforts to see their kids. And Mr. Schafer and Dawn are even separated by three thousand miles.

What else about me? I think boys are dweebs, except for Bart, Logan (Mary Anne's boyfriend), and the boys I sit for. I even think my fifteen-year-old brother Sam is a dweeb. I like animals and we have a puppy named Shannon (after my friend Shannon), and an old cat of Watson's named Boo-Boo. Sometimes I think my house is a zoo, but I like the activity.

So there you are. You have just met my friends and me. I know I'm lucky to have such good friends. I also know I'm lucky to have a family, even a mixed-up one. I knew that when Emily came into the den holding out a sneaker I'd lost and said proudly, "Soo." (Shoe). I gave her a big hug.

CHAPTER 3

"Thanks, Charlie!"

"See you in half an hour," he replied.

It was almost time for a Monday club meeting and Charlie had just dropped me off at Claudia's in his "car." (Now that I live in a different neighborhood, Charlie has to drive me to and from BSC meetings. The club pays him to do this.)

I ran to Claudia's front door and right on inside, without bothering to ring the bell. There was no point. I knew Claud was probaby the only Kishi at home, and anyway, we club members never ring the bell.

"Hi, Claud!" I greeted her, as I entered her room. (I am always relieved when her sister, Janine, isn't home. Janine is nice enough, I guess, but she's forever correcting your grammar and vocabulary. I guess that comes with being the genius that she is.)

"Hi," replied Claud. She was lying on her

21

bed, reading *The Clue of the Velvet Mask*, and one of her legs was propped up on a pillow.

"I guess it's going to rain, huh?" I said.

Claud broke her leg awhile ago and ever since, it has hurt her when it's going to rain. It's a pretty good barometer.

"Yeah," agreed Claud. "Do you think Dawn and the others will mind sitting on the floor with Jessi and Mal today? My leg *really* hurts."

"Nope," I replied. "Is there any junk food you want me to search for?"

"Hmm." Claud closed her Nancy Drew book with a snap and looked thoughtful. "Try — Oh, wait a sec. There's something right here." She reached under the comforter that was lumpily folded at the foot of her bed and retrieved a bag of potato chips and a package of Gummi Bears. "These'll do," she said.

"I'll pass them around," I told her.

Mary Anne and Dawn arrived then, so I took my presidential seat in Claudia's director's chair, put on the visor I wear at meetings, and stuck a pencil over one ear.

"Hi, guys," I said.

"Hi," they replied. They were already settling themselves on the floor.

Usually Claudia, Mary Anne, and Dawn sit on the bed, Stacey sits in Claudia's desk chair (or sometimes Dawn sits in the chair and Stacey sits on the bed), Jessi and Mal sit on the floor, and I sit where I was already sitting, in the place of honor. (The director's chair makes me feel tall.) Today, Stacey would probably sit at the desk, and the floor would just be a little more crowded than usual.

I looked at Claudia's digital alarm clock, which is the official BSC timepiece. As soon as those numbers change from 5:29 to 5:30, the meeting begins, even if a club member hasn't arrived. I'm a stickler for being on time, though, so my friends are hardly ever late.

Our club meets three times a week, on Mondays, Wednesdays, and Fridays, from five-thirty until six. As president, I try to run it professionally. But let me back up here and tell you how the club started, before I tell you how it works.

See, at the beginning of seventh grade, long before so many things had changed, I still lived here on Bradford Court, across the street from Claud. David Michael was only six then, and since Mom worked full-time, Sam and Charlie and I took turns baby-sitting for him after school. (I baby-sat for other kids, too, though.) Anyway, of course a day came when none of us — not Charlie, not Sam, not I — could sit for our little brother. So Mom started calling baby-sitters. It was while I was eating

23

a piece of pizza and watching Mom on the phone that it occurred to me that my mother could save a lot of time if she could make just one call and reach a lot of sitters, instead of making all those separate calls. So I got together with Mary Anne and Claud, told them my idea, and we began the BSC!

The first thing we decided was that we needed another club member, so we asked Stacey to join. She had just moved here from New York and was getting to be friends with Claudia. Stacey was dying to join, and the club was a success from the beginning. (We advertised a lot — by word of mouth, with fliers, even with an ad in our local paper.) Soon we had so much business that we needed a new member, so we asked Dawn, who was Mary Anne's new friend at the time, to join. Then Stacey moved back to New York, we replaced her with Mal and Jessi, and *then* Stacey returned to Stoneybrook. We have seven members now, and I think that's enough. Claudia's room is getting crowded.

Here's how we run the club and what our responsibilities are:

I am the president, as you know. It's my job to keep the BSC in good shape and fresh by coming up with new ideas. (Besides, I thought up the club in the first place.) Some of my ideas are Kid-Kits, the club notebook, and the club record book. Kid-Kits are cartons (we each have one) that we decorated with Claudia's art materials and filled with our old toys, games, and books, as well as some new things, such as coloring books, sticker books, Magic Markers, etc. We sometimes take the kits on jobs with us, and our charges love them. This is good business, because when our charges are happy, then their parents are happy, and when parents are happy, they call the Baby-sitters Club with more jobs for us!

The record book is Mary Anne's and Stacey's department, so I'll describe that later, but let me explain about the notebook. The notebook is more like a diary. In it, each of us is responsible for writing up every single job we go on. This is a chore, but it's helpful because we also have to read the diary once a week to see what went on during our friends' recent jobs. We learn about problems our charges are having, how to solve tough sitting situations, and that sort of thing.

Now let's see. Claudia is our vice-president. This is because she has her own phone *and* her own personal phone number, so her room is an ideal place to hold meetings. Thanks to our advertising, our clients know when the BSC gets together so they call us during meetings. We spend a lot of time on the phone and don't have to worry about tying up our parents' lines. Thank goodness for Claud and her phone.

Mary Anne is our secretary and she has a pretty big job. Remember the record book I mentioned? Well, Mary Anne is in charge of it (except for the numbers section, which is Stacey's domain). In the record book, Mary Anne has noted all of our clients, their phone numbers, addresses, the rates they pay, the number of children they have, etc. More important are the appointment pages. There, Mary Anne writes down all the jobs we have lined up and who's got the jobs. She's great at this. I don't know how she does it, because she has to keep track of so many schedules — Jessi's ballet classes, Claud's art lessons, plus eye doctor and dentist appointments, and more. But she's great at it. She's never made a mistake. (Also, she has the neatest handwriting of any club member.)

As treasurer, Stacey collects our weekly dues on Mondays. She's a whiz at math. (I hate to admit it, but where math is concerned, she's almost as smart as Janine, Claud's sister.) Anyway, Stacey collects the dues, puts it in the treasury (a manila envelope), makes sure the treasury doesn't get too low, and doles out the money when it's needed. (Stacey *loves* collecting and having money, even when it isn't, technically speaking, her own — and hates parting with it.) The dues money goes to Charlie to drive me to and from meetings, helps Claud pay her monthly phone bill, buys things for our Kid-Kits when we run out of them, and every now and then covers the cost of a club pizza party or overnight. Stacey also keeps track of how much money we earn. She does this in the record book. It's just for our own information, since we each keep whatever we earn on a job. We don't pool the money or anything.

Dawn is our alternate officer, which means that she's a sort of substitute teacher. She takes on the job of anyone who has to miss a meeting. We don't miss meetings often, but Dawn's job can be hard since she has to know everyone's duties. However, she doesn't have much to do at most meetings so we let her answer the phone a lot.

Jessi and Mal are junior officers. That means that they can only baby-sit after school or on weekend days. They aren't allowed to sit at night yet unless they're sitting for their own brothers and sisters. They're a huge help to us, though. Not only are they good, responsible, reliable sitters, but they free up us older club members for evening jobs.

Last of all are two associate members who don't attend meetings. They are my friend Shannon Kilbourne and Mary Anne's boyfriend, Logan. Shannon and Logan are our backups. They are good baby-sitters who can pinch-hit in case a job is offered for a time when all seven of us regular sitters are busy. I know that sounds unlikely, but it *does* happen. The associate members don't attend meetings, Shannon because she's too busy with other activities, and Logan because he's embarrassed to sit around in a girl's room for half an hour three times a week. It's one thing for him to join us at our lunch table in the cafeteria. There, he can escape if he wants to. But when he's in Claud's room, he feels stuck.

Anyway, that's the BSC.

I had been keeping my eye on Claud's clock, and when the numbers turned to 5:30, I cleared my throat. Everyone had arrived and it was time to start the meeting.

"Treasurer," I said, "please collect the dues."

With a look of glee, Stacey handed around the manila envelope, and each of us dropped a one-dollar bill in it. Most of us groaned as we did so. Even me.

Then Stacey dumped the contents of the envelope onto Claud's desk, counted it up, and announced that the treasury contained more than twenty dollars.

"Well, fork over," I said. "I've got to pay Charlie today."

Stacey looked pained but gave me the money.

"And I need some stuff for my Kid-Kit," said Dawn. "The Magic Markers have dried up, and someone — I'm not sure who, but I'm betting on Jenny Prezzioso — scribbled on every page of a new coloring book."

"Barbie's head fell off," reported Jessi. "I need a new Barbie doll."

Everyone laughed. We knew she was just kidding.

The first phone call of the day came in then, and Dawn took it.

"Hello, Baby-sitters Club," she said. "Oh, hi, Mrs. Kuhn."

The Kuhns are not regular clients of the BSC, but the Kuhn kids are on my Krushers team, so Mrs. Kuhn does call for a sitter every now and then. Mary Anne arranged for Mal to take an afternoon job with them.

As soon as Dawn had called Mrs. Kuhn back to tell her who would be baby-sitting, the phone rang again. And again and again and again. It was one of our busiest meetings ever.

Mmm. I just love busy meetings.

One of the last calls was from Mrs. Pike, Mal's mother, needing two sitters (she always insists on two sitters, since there are so many Pike kids) for a Saturday afternoon. Mary Anne arranged the job for Mal and Jessi. We usually let each other sit for our own brothers and sisters, if possible. We're pretty nice about doling out the jobs. Not much fighting goes on.

At six o'clock, we took what Claudia hoped was the last call of the meeting. (If a client calls after six, poor Claudia has to deal with things on her own. That's one of the problems that comes with having your own phone number. On the other hand, Claud can talk up a storm in private, while the rest of us have to hide out in closets during personal calls, hoping nobody is listening in on an extension.)

As soon as Dawn hung up the phone, my friends and I said good-bye to Claud and left. Charlie was waiting for me. He demanded his money before he would drive me home.

CHAPTER 4

When Charlie and I walked in the front door of our house, I was greeted by David Michael, who said, "Shannon called *four* times while you were gone! She said to phone her as soon as you get home. She says it's really, really, really important."

"What's important?" I asked my brother.

"She wouldn't tell me. She just said for you to call her."

So I did. Immediately. In case it was private, I took our cordless phone into a closet we hardly ever use and called Shannon from there. The connection wasn't so hot, even with the phone antenna stretched as far as it would go, but at least we could hear each other.

"Shannon?" I said when she got on the phone.

"Kristy? Is that you?"

Crackle, crackle. (Static.) "Yeah. What's going on?"

"You sound like you're calling from a tunnel."

"I'm on the cordless phone in a closet. David Michael made your phone message sound so mysterious I thought I better hide, just in case."

"Oh. Well, listen. You won't believe this. I forgot to get our mail until really late this afternoon." (Shannon's parents both work, so it's up to Shannon and her sisters, Tiffany and Maria, to get the mail after school. Sometimes nobody remembers until after *dinner*.) "Anyway, it was a lucky thing *I* got the mail, because there was an envelope in it for you."

"So?" I said, puzzled. "The mailman stuck it in the wrong box."

"The mailman didn't deliver it," said Shannon, with some satisfaction. "There's no stamp or postmark on it. There's not even an address. It just says 'Kristy,' and there are heart stickers and flower stickers all over it."

Crackle, crackle. "You're kidding," I said in a hushed voice.

"It looks like a love letter," Shannon added tantalizingly.

"A" (*crackle*) "me? No way. No one has" (*crackle*) "love" (*crackle*).

"Kristy, would you get out of that closet or

32

off that phone? I can't understand a word you're saying."

"I'm not leaving the closet." (*Crackle*.) "If my brothers hear about — "

"Kristy!" It was Mom calling me.

"Shannon, I have to go. Can you" (*crackle*) "over after supper?"

"Can I bring the letter over after supper? Sure. I don't know how long I can stay, but I'm dying to know what's in this envelope. . . . That is, if you'll let me see. You will let me see, won't you?"

"I guess so." (*Crackle*.) "I mean, it'll de — " (*crackle*) "what the letter, or whatever it is, says. It might be very personal."

"KRISTY!" That time Sam was calling me. He's got the world's loudest voice. It's like a sonic boom.

"I really have to go now," I told Shannon. "See you later. And thanks."

Shannon and I hung up. I pushed down the antenna on the cordless phone, burst out of the closet, and flew into the kitchen. I knew I was late for dinner.

"Sorry," I said, as I slid into my place on the bench. (We eat at a long table with a bench at either side and Emily's high chair at one end.) "I *had* to talk to Shannon. She's going to come over after dinner. She won't stay long," I added quickly. "We both have homework." We hadn't said that over the phone, but we always have homework, so why should that night have been any different?

Somehow, I got through dinner. I really don't know how I did it. All I could think of was the envelope and the hearts and flowers.

I am not the hearts-and-flowers type.

At seven-thirty, our bell rang.

"I'll get it!" I screeched. I half expected Watson to say, "Indoor voice, Kristy," to me, which is what we have to say to Karen a lot. She tends to get noisy.

By now, David Michael was as curious as I was about what was going on. He'd taken the messages from Shannon. He knew I'd called Shannon from inside the closet. And now he saw that I couldn't *wait* for Shannon to come inside. So he was right next to me when I answered the door.

"Hi," I said breathlessly.

There stood Shannon. She has thick, curly, blonde hair (similar to Stacey's) and blue eyes, but I wouldn't call her gorgeous like Dawn or even attractive like Stacey. She's more . . . interesting-looking. I once heard someone say that being called "interesting" is practically a curse. It's the word people use when they don't want to say someone's ugly. But I don't agree. At least not in Shannon's case. She really *is* interesting-looking. She has high cheekbones, like that actress Meryl Streep, and wide eyes. Her lashes are very pale, but she's allowed to use makeup, so she puts on black mascara every morning. And she has a ski-jump nose, the kind that's almost too cute. (Shannon told me once that she wants a nose job — to straighten it out — but her parents say no. They aren't strict. They just think she should wait until she's an adult before she makes a decision like that.)

I let Shannon inside. She was still wearing her Stoneybrook Day School uniform. Shannon, Bart, and about half the kids in our neighborhood go to Stoneybrook Day School. Karen, Andrew, and a lot of other kids go to another private school called Stoneybrook Academy. My brothers and I are practically the only kids around here who go to public school.

"So?" I said eagerly to Shannon.

She pulled the envelope out of the pocket of her school uniform and handed it to me. I was so excited I could hardly breathe. Then I realized that David Michael was at my elbow.

"Let's go to my room," I said hastily. Shannon and I thundered up the stairs. David Michael was at our heels.

When we reached the door to my room and I realized that we were still a trio, I had to say, "David Michael, this is private. You can't come in." (I couldn't help being blunt. I was nearing hysteria.)

"But I want to know what's going on," he said.

"Maybe I'll tell you later," I replied "*Maybe*. Anyway, this is girl stuff." I knew that would get him.

"*Girl* stuff! Gross. Forget it. I don't want to know after all."

I grinned at Shannon. David Michael had taken off like a shot.

Shannon and I darted into my room and I closed the door behind us. We flopped on my bed, and I let the envelope dangle between my thumb and forefinger.

Then we examined the envelope together. The front said simply KRISTY. The word was typed but the "I" had been dotted with a tiny heart sticker. A flower sticker had been placed carefully in each corner of the envelope.

"Maybe it's not for me," I said. "It doesn't say 'Kristy Thomas.' It just says 'Kristy.'"

36

"Well, there aren't any Kristys at my house," Shannon replied. "And I can't think of any other Kristys in the neighborhood — and I know practically everyone around here."

I turned the envelope over. On the back were more hearts and flowers. All I could do was stare at the envelope.

"Well, open it before I die!" cried Shannon.

I ripped the envelope open. Suddenly I felt shy. "Let me read it first," I said to Shannon. "It might be embarrassing."

Shannon understood. "Okay." She rolled over and closed her eyes.

I read the note inside. Compared to the envelope, it was very plain. It was typewritten (or maybe word-processed) on white paper. The note said, "Dear Kristy, I think you are beautiful. And you're the nicest girl I know. I would like to go steady with you. I wish I could tell you this in person. Love, Your Mystery Admirer."

I sat up. "Well, it's not too bad," I said. "Here." I handed the note to Shannon. "What do you think?"

Shannon read the note and smiled, saying, "You've got a *mystery* admirer! That is so romantic."

I was surprised. Shannon is almost as sophisticated as Stacey. She's had millions of boyfriends and gone out on plenty of dates. Plus she gets to wear that makeup. It's hard to believe we're the same age. And here she was, all gooey over a little note.

"I bet it's Sam," I said. "It's one of his practical jokes."

"Why would he put the note in *our* mailbox?" asked Shannon.

"To throw me off the track," I replied. "That's why he couldn't use his own handwriting."

"You are such a dweeb," she said. "You know it's from Bart."

"Bart! Why wouldn't Bart tell me those things in person?"

"They aren't so easy to say," Shannon told me. She sounded as if she were speaking from experience.

"But you just said I have a mystery admirer. Why are you so excited if you think you know who the mystery admirer is?"

"Because. It's still romantic."

"Okay. Then why are there hearts and flowers all over the envelope? Stacey McGill is the only person I know who dots 'I's' with hearts. Boys don't do that. This looks like it's from a girl."

"A girl who wants to go steady with you?

Kristy, grow up. Bart just wanted to make the envelope look nice."

"All right. How about *this?* Why did Bart, who knows perfectly well where I live, put the envelope in your mailbox?"

Shannon frowned. "That one I can't answer. But anyway, who else would send you a note like this? Can you think of anyone?"

I couldn't. Except for Sam.

"Listen, I have to go," said Shannon. "I have a huge history paper due next week. Why don't you call Bart? Maybe he'll drop a hint about the note."

"Okay," I answered. I walked Shannon downstairs. Then I got on the phone in the kitchen. I figured that if I made another cordless-phone-in-the-closet call, it would arouse suspicion.

Bart's little brother answered the phone. When I asked for Bart, he yelled, "BART!" and dropped the phone and walked away.

"Sorry about that," said Bart. "We've got to work on Kyle's manners. What's up?"

"Not much," I replied. "How's the band?"

"It's fine. We still don't have a place to practice, though."

Bart and I talked for about fifteen minutes. We talked a lot about his band. Then we talked about a teacher at my school that I don't like much, and about a couple of other things.

But Bart did not mention the mystery note and neither did I. When we got off the phone, I was not at all convinced that Bart was my mystery admirer, even if Shannon thought so. But if he wasn't, then who was?

CHAPTER 5

Tuesday

Today the Krushers held a practice, and I was baby-sitting for the Perkins girls, so I took them over to the field. Myriah and Gabbie helped me push Laura in her stroller. They are so good with their baby sister-- and with each other. I don't see too many brothers and sisters who are as close as they are. It makes me wish I had a sister.

Anyway, there's not much to say about the afternoon. It was pretty uneventful. Kristy was in charge of the Krushers, which included Myriah and Gabbie, so I just sat with Laura. We sat in the shade because it's not good for babies (or anyone, really) to get too much sun. Laura took a long nap. While she slept, I talked to Shannon, who had turned up to watch softball practice. Then I took the girls home. That's about it, you guys!

Oh, yeah -- Shannon is really nice.

What a day Tuesday was for me. Stacey's afternoon was pretty tame, judging from her notebook entry, but my whole day was, well, surprising.

It started when I leaned out of our front door very early in the morning to bring in the newspaper and found another envelope addressed to me. It was lying on the doormat, right next to the paper. (We have a very accurate paper girl. She hits the front steps every time. Either she has fantastic aim, or she *walks* the paper to the door.)

I grabbed the paper and the note, dropped the newspaper on the kitchen table, and then ran to my room with the envelope. I wasn't even dressed yet, but I read the letter right away, then thought it over while I got ready for school.

The envelope wasn't as fancy as the first one had been. It just said KRISTY on the front, and the back flap was sealed with a pink heart sticker. I kind of wished the "I" in my name

42

had been dotted with a heart again. Anyway, inside was another typed note. This one said, "Dearest Kristy, I can't stop thinking about you. Maybe I'm in love with you. I don't know. I've never been in love before. You are as beautiful as a snow-covered mountain. Love, Your Mystery Admirer."

Well, that last part was a little flowery (overwritten, my English teacher would say), but I didn't care. I'm not sure anyone had ever called me beautiful, except maybe Mom, and that doesn't count, because all mothers say their children are beautiful.

Of course, I told my friends about the notes while we ate lunch in the cafeteria that day. And, like Shannon, they were all sure Bart was my mystery admirer. I seemed to be the only one with any doubts.

Okay, so I had gotten a letter in the morning. Imagine my surprise when I found *another* one in our mailbox that afternoon. It said simply, "Dear Kristy, I love you, I love you, I love you. Love (get the picture?), Your Mystery Admirer."

I was floating on air by the time Shannon and I got to the ball field for the Krushers practice that day. And that was only the beginning of my excitement.

                    * * *

Stacey, meanwhile, went straight to the Perkinses' after school. She was greeted at the
door by an exuberant Myriah and Gabbie.
(Myriah is five-and-a-half, and Gabbie is almost three. Guess what. Their family moved
into our house when *we* moved into Watson's
house!)

"Toshe me up, Stacey McGill! Toshe me
up!" cried Gabbie. (That's Gabbie-talk for
"Pick me up and give me a hug.") So Stacey
toshed her up. When she set her down, Myriah grinned and said, "I'm learning how to
ride a bike with no training wheels!"

She was very proud of herself.

A few minutes later, Mrs. Perkins left.

"Ready for your Krushers practice?" Stacey
asked Myriah and Gabbie.

"Yes!" they cried. They were wearing pants,
sneakers, and their special Krushers T-shirts.

"You need hats," Stacey reminded them.
"You're going to be in the sun all afternoon."
The girls dutifully found two old baseball caps,
while Stacey tied a little pink hat on Laura and
put her *very* distant fedora on her own head.
Then they set off.

Gabbie and Myriah took turns helping Stacey push Laura's stroller. When they reached
the practice field, the older girls ran to me.

44

Stacey took Laura to a grassy spot under a tree and sat next to the stroller.

"Do you want to sit on my lap?" she started to say to the baby, when she realized that Laura had fallen sound asleep. Well, thought Stacey, *this* will be an easy sitting job.

She was settling down with a book she'd brought along in case this happened, when I left my Krushers and ran over to her.

"Stacey!" I cried. "I got a *third* note this afternoon." I told her what it said, and Stacey just grinned.

"Hey, Kristy," a voice said.

Stacey peered around me and saw Shannon Kilbourne. She'd met Shannon a few times, so she knew her slightly. "Hi!" said Stacey.

"Hi," Shannon replied. "Listen, Kristy, your kids are getting a little zooey. I think you ought to start the practice."

So I did. I left Shannon and Stacey together under the tree with Laura. I hoped they would talk. I wanted Shannon and the other BSC members to know each other better.

They did talk.

"I've never seen you at a Krushers practice before," said Stacey amiably to Shannon. (She checked on Laura, who was still asleep.)

"I usually don't have time to come," Shannon replied. "Just like I can't come to the Baby-sitters Club meetings. I'm either at school in the afternoons — I'm in a lot of clubs — or I have to watch Maria, my youngest sister, or I'm baby-sitting somewhere else. But today I'm *free!* So I thought I'd come support the Krushers. A bunch of the kids I sit for are on the team. Kristy's great with them."

"How old is Maria?" Stacey asked. "Is she on the team?"

"Maria's eight. And no, she's not on the team. She hates anything athletic. Can you believe it? She *likes* doing homework."

Stacey smiled. "I know someone like that. Charlotte Johanssen. She's eight, too. But she's one of the Krushers cheerleaders, so she'll try athletic stuff sometimes. She's right over there." (Stacey pointed.) "I love that kid. She's almost like a sister to me."

Practice had begun and it was going well, from the actual playing to the cheerleading. Jamie Newton even put his hand out when the ball sailed toward him instead of ducking. He didn't catch the ball, but at least he tried. Claire struck out and did not have a tantrum. Overall, the kids on both of the teams into which I had divided the Krushers, hit very well. Plus, the two main pitchers, David Michael and Nicky Pike (one of Mal's brothers) were really improving.

When practice was over, Stacey and Shannon stood up and cheered, along with Charlotte, Vanessa, and Haley.

"Good game," said Shannon to Stacey and Mal (who was sitting for the Kuhn kids).

I trotted over to my friends as the Krushers started to leave. "You know what?" I said breathlessly. "I think we could beat the Bashers again — even with*out* handicaps."

"The kids are improving, that's for sure," said Stacey, as Gabbie and Myriah ran to her and checked on their little sister.

"Ooh, she's sleeping," said Gabbie in a hushed voice. "Quiet, everyone."

I could tell that Stacey and Shannon and Mal wanted to laugh (I did), but instead we just lowered our voices.

"I better get going," said Shannon. "I'm supposed to start dinner tonight."

"I'm glad you guys had a chance to talk," I said.

"Me, too," replied Stacey. She smiled at Shannon. Then she left with the Perkins girls, Gabbie tiptoeing across the grass so as not to disturb Laura.

Later that afternoon, Stacey received a call from me.

"Hi," I said. "How was the rest of your sitting job?"

"Oh, fine. The girls were angels," Stacey reported. "Laura woke up on the way back and Myriah and Gabbie entertained her with songs until we reached their house. Mrs. Perkins was already home, so I left then."

"Well, guess what. Just as you guys were heading away from the ball field, Bart showed up. He walked me home again. And you will never guess what we have decided to do."

"Elope?" said Stacey.

"No!" I was horrified.

"I was just kidding. I mean, because of the mystery admirer stuff."

"Oh. Well, anyway, we decided to hold a *World Series* between the Krushers and the Bashers."

"Really?"

"Yeah."

"How many games will you play?"

"Well, we had sort of a fight over that," I admitted. "I wanted to play three games, but Bart said one was enough for little kids. He thought three would be too much pressure, especially for kids like Claire Pike. I still don't agree with him, but I gave in. At least our fight is over."

"*That's* good," said Stacey. "Did Bart give away anything about being your mystery admirer?"

"Not a thing. That's why I'm so sure he's not the one."

"But he *has* to be," said Stacey.

"You sound like Shannon."

"I can't help it. Bart makes the most sense."

I started to tell her all the reasons why I knew Bart *wasn't* my mystery admirer, but I was tired of repeating them. Instead, I said, "I did something you won't believe."

"What?"

"I asked Bart to the Halloween Hop at our school and he said he'd come." That announcement was greeted by such a long silence that I said, "Stacey? . . . Stace? . . . Are you there?"

Finally she burst out laughing. "I'm here," she replied. "I really *can't* believe you did that! That's great. The Hop's coming up in just a couple of weeks — but you'll have to find something to wear, and fix your hair, and . . ."

Stacey was off and running. I think she was more excited than I was.

"This," I said, "is completely gross." I poked at something yellowy-brown on the plate of food I'd just bought in the hot-lunch line in the cafeteria.

"Then *why*," said Claudia, "did you buy the hot lunch? You could buy a sandwich or a salad, you know."

I shrugged.

Claud, Stacey, Mary Anne, Dawn, Logan, and I were sitting at our usual table in the school cafeteria. (Mal and Jessi eat during another period since they're not in our grade.)

"Besides," I said, stabbing the unrecognizable thing with my fork, holding it up, and letting it dangle in front of me, "I like to gross out Mary Anne." I aimed my fork in her direction.

"Put it *down!*" shrieked Mary Anne, and Logan gave me a dirty look, which wasn't really very dirty.

"Of all the people at this table," said Dawn, "who would think that *she*" (Dawn pointed at me) "would have a mystery admirer?" Dawn looked as grossed out as Mary Anne.

"Or that she'd be the *president* of the BSC," added Stacey. "Kristy, either put that thing down or eat it."

I put it down. I certainly wasn't about to eat it.

We talked about baby-sitting for awhile. Mary Anne said that prissy Mrs. Prezzioso had actually bought Jenny a pair of pants. Until now, it had been hard to distinguish Jenny from lace curtains. Then Mal said that Matt Braddock was going to be in a play in his special school. The entire performance would be done in sign language. It was going to be a Halloween play.

Halloween reminded me of the Halloween Hop, and we began to talk about who was going with whom, and who was just going to go and hope for the best. Mary Anne and Logan were going together, of course. Claudia was hoping that this boy, Woody Jefferson, would ask her. Stacey was trying to get up the nerve to ask some new boy in her English class to go with her, and Dawn said she would go alone.

"A lot of kids do that," she added defensively. Then she said that she thought I was so brave to have asked Bart. (By that time, everyone knew what I'd done. Secrets don't last long in the BSC.)

"Speaking of Bart," said Mary Anne. "Have you gotten any more notes?"

"Another one this morning!" I replied.

"And you didn't *tell* us?" cried Claudia. (You have to have a loud voice to be heard in our cafeteria.)

"Sorry," I replied. "It was the fourth one. I guess I'm getting used to them."

"*Used* to them!" repeated Dawn, awed.

"Boy, if I had a mystery admirer who was sending me love letters — " Stacey began loudly.

"SHH! Keep your voice down!" I said.

"If I keep my voice down, you won't be able to hear me," replied Stacey.

That was true, but I had noticed that Cokie Mason and her snobby little crowd — Grace Blume and two other girls, Lisa and Bebe — were sitting at the next table. They were being awfully quiet.

"You guys," I whispered, and my friends leaned forward to hear me.

"Is this going to be girl talk?" Logan whispered back.

"Sort of," I replied.

"See ya." Logan stood up abruptly and left. He hates when our conversations become too "girlish."

"I brought the letters with me. Look." I spread the notes out on the table. I had even saved the envelopes because I liked the stickers on them.

Mary Anne, Dawn, Claud, and Stacey bunched around the letters.

" 'I love you, I love you, I love you,' " Mary Anne read. She sighed. "That is so, so romantic."

"Distant," added Claudia.

"But you guys don't really think they're from — " I stopped. We had an audience. The boys at one table were watching us with great curiosity, and at the next table, Cokie Mason was peering rudely at us. Then she turned to Grace and snickered.

I put the letters away in a hurry.

"Don't pay any attention to Cokie and those guys," said Stacey.

"Yeah. They're probably jealous. I bet none of them ever got a love note from a secret admirer," said Mary Anne.

"I wonder why the letters are all typed," Stacey was saying.

"SHH!" (I hissed it.) "I already told you. It's so the mystery admirer can disguise his hand-writing."

"Then they *must* be from Bart Taylor. Who else would *need* to disguise his writing?"

"Sam," I said.

Cokie and her friends got up then and left the cafeteria. They didn't even bother to clear off the table they'd been sitting at.

"What pigs," I said.

As you can tell, we do not like Cokie and her group very much. And we have good reason not to.

"Remember Halloween?" spoke up Mary Anne, just as I was about to say the same thing. I guess that's a sign of being best friends.

"Boy, do I ever," said Claudia.

"What? What happened on Halloween?" asked Stacey. (She'd been back in New York then.)

"Mary Anne started getting these weird, threatening notes. Someone even sent her a bad-luck charm. And then, we really did have bad luck. We thought we were . . . well, I'm not sure what we thought," said Claudia falteringly, "but anyway, it turned out that Cokie and her friends were behind everything. They wanted to make us look like jerks, because they liked Logan and wanted him to hang around with them — not with jerks."

"So what happened?" asked Stacey.

"*We* made *them* look like jerks. And we did it in the middle of the graveyard at midnight on Halloween."

"Don't ask what possessed us." Dawn giggled. "Get it? *Possessed* us?"

We laughed.

"I really don't know where we found the courage to do that, but we did," I said. "Mal and Jessi were with us. The BSC sticks together."

The five of us were silent for a few moments, thinking, I guess, about Cokie and Logan and Halloween. Then the bell rang. Lunch was over. *We* cleaned up our table before we left the cafeteria.

That afternoon I baby-sat for David Michael and Emily. As usual, Mom and Watson were at work, Charlie and Sam were at after-school sports, and Nannie had bowling practice. Nannie is in a senior citizens league. They play really well. Nannie even has a trophy in her bedroom.

Nannie is a character and I love her. We all do. Emily Michelle is especially attached to her. In fact, she cried as she and David Michael

55

and I stood at the front door and watched Nannie drive off in the Pink Clinker. (That's Nannie's old car, and it really is pink. Nannie had it painted pink on purpose because she likes the color.)

"Come on, Emily," I said as I closed the door. "Nannie will be back soon. She has to practice her bowling."

"Yeah, you want her to be a champ, don't you?" asked David Michael.

"Cookie," Emily replied pathetically.

"Boy, she sure learns fast, doesn't she?" I said to my brother. "Okay, one cookie, Emily. Just one."

"Can I have one, too?" asked David Michael. He made a sad face. "I miss Nannie. A cookie will make me feel better."

I punched him playfully on the arm and he grinned.

The three of us were just finishing our snack when the doorbell rang. "I'll get it," I said. "David Michael, keep an eye on Emily, okay?"

My brother nodded.

I ran to the front door, opened it, and saw nobody. But a note was lying next to the mat. My heart began to pound. Another letter from my mystery admirer! I grabbed it up and read it before I'd even closed the door. When I'd finished, my heart was still pounding, because this note was . . . weird. It said, "I love you, I love you, I love you, but beware. Love is fickle. So are friends. Watch out for your mystery admirer."

Of course I called Shannon immediately, praying that for once she'd be home after school and able to come over. She was and she did. While David Michael and Emily played and watched TV, Shannon and I discussed the note. We examined every angle. We read it and reread it.

"I hate to admit it, but maybe I was wrong," said Shannon shakily. "This couldn't be from Bart. This note is sort of . . . *twisted*."

"What if it *is* from Bart?" I asked. "Maybe he's crazy."

"He's not crazy! I go to school with him. I ought to know. Maybe somebody else sent it."

"No. It looks just like the others."

"How come you're so willing to believe Bart is your mystery admirer all of a sudden?" asked Shannon.

"I'm not. I mean, I don't know. But if he *is*, then I've invited a psycho to the Halloween Hop."

CHAPTER 7

Saturday

Today Jessi and I sat for my brothers and sisters.

And, boy, is Halloween in the air.

I'll say. That's all we heard about this afternoon.

But it was fun, wasn't it?

Yeah. I kind of wished I could still make a costume and go out trick-or-treating, collecting candy.

You're off the track, Mal.

Oh, yeah. Anyway, the kids spent the entire afternoon on Halloween projects. They're going to set up a haunted house in our basement.

And charge money for it, I might add.

Oh, well. But this will interest you, Kristy. Vanessa got an idea that involves the Krushers, their World Series, and Halloween....

Mallory and Jessi *did* have a fun afternoon. It started right after lunch, as Jessi was arriving at Mal's house, and Mr. and Mrs. Pike were leaving.

Claire was running around with a clown mask on her face, calling everyone a silly-billy-goo-goo, when Margo said, "Maybe I'll be a clown for Halloween this year."

"Oh, that is so ordinary," retorted Vanessa, who is nine and plans to be a poet one day.

"Well, what are *you* going to be?" asked Margo. (Margo is seven.)

"A poet," replied Vanessa in a superior voice.

"What does a poet look like?" wondered Nicky. (He's eight.) But he didn't wonder for long. "*I* better think of a costume," he added.

"We all better," said Byron, one of the ten-year-old triplets.

"I'm going to be a giraffe," said Claire.

"In your dreams," replied Jordan (another triplet). "How would you be a giraffe? How would you see? You would have to stretch your neck out about ten feet to get your head under a giraffe mask."

Mal and Jessi laughed. They were sitting with the kids in the Pikes' rec room. The day was dreary and no one felt like going outside.

"I will wear the giraffe neck on my head," said Claire haughtily. "I'll make little eyeholes in the neck so I can see out."

"You have to admit that's clever," said Adam, the third triplet.

The Pike kids looked impressed.

"I'm going to be a hobo this year," spoke up Nicky.

"Lame," said Jordan. "I'm going to be a mummy."

"I suppose no one's ever been a mummy before," said Mal, eyeing her brother.

Jordan made a face. Then he brightened. "I know. I'll be a *head*less mummy. Now *that's* original!"

"I wonder what I can do to look like a poet," mused Vanessa.

"Dress up like a pen?" suggested Margo.

"No, I want to look like a poet. I mean, a poetess." She paused. "Mallory? Do poetesses wear berets on their heads and look raggedy?"

"Nope. Those are starving artists," replied Mal.

The triplets began to rifle through the Pikes' box of dress-up clothes and props. They pulled out hats and masks and a doctor's bag. Then Adam found a spool of thread. A simple spool of thread.

"What's that doing in there?" asked Jessi.

"I don't know," Adam answered, "but I just got a *great* idea."

"What?" asked the others.

"You guys, we should make a haunted house in our basement. We'll set it up on Halloween — that's a Saturday — and during the day, kids can come through it. We'll have ghosts and moving things and lots of scary stuff. We can use the thread for cobwebs. We'll charge ten cents or maybe twenty-five cents apiece. Everyone will get their money's worth!"

"That," replied Jordan, "really is a great idea."

"Can we all help?" asked Nicky. (Sometimes the triplets do things on their own. And they often leave Nicky out, even though he's the only other boy in the Pike household.)

But — "Sure, you can all help," said Adam surprisingly. "We'll need lots of people. We'll need someone to answer the door and take kids down to the basement. We'll need someone else to lead each kid through the haunted house. And we'll need dressed-up people, like ghosts and *headless mummies* to walk around. Real people are scarier than fake ones."

"You know what else?" said Vanessa. (She

was about to make a very un-Vanessa-like suggestion.) "There should be a part of the haunted house where we blindfold people. Then we make them put their hands in peeled grapes and cold spaghetti and stuff. We'll tell them the grapes are eyeballs and the spaghetti is brains. They will be so grossed out!"

"Vanessa, you're a genius!" exclaimed Jordan.

"Not really," she replied modestly. "I saw it on TV."

"Well, anyway, we'll definitely do that," said Jordan.

"And we'll play a haunted-house sound effects tape," added Adam. "The kids will hear moaning and groaning and screaming and doors slamming and the wind howling and thunder and everything!" Adam was all worked up.

Claire looked a little scared, but she covered up her feelings. She didn't want to be left out of the family project.

The Pike kids fell into silence. Their thoughts must have drifted from Halloween, because the next thing that was said was, "Do you think we can really beat the Bashers?" (That was Nicky.)

"In the World Series?" asked Margo.

Nicky nodded. "What do you think, Mallory?"

"I don't know. You beat them before, but I think you'll have to try very hard not to be nervous during the big game."

"And the cheerleaders will try very hard to . . . to, um . . . to lead the Krushers to victory," said Vanessa dramatically. "Hey! I've got an idea. Since the World Series game will be played right before Halloween, Charlotte and Haley and I should wear costumes. I mean, Halloween costumes."

"That would be cool," said Nicky. Then he looked out the window. "It isn't raining, Mallory. Can Claire and Margo and I practice catching and hitting in the backyard?"

"Sure," replied Mallory.

The kids split up then. The three younger ones went outside. The triplets began planning the spook house. And Vanessa got on the phone with her fellow cheerleaders to discuss costumes. She called Haley first.

"Hi, Haley. It's Vanessa. Listen, I've got this idea." She explained her plan to Haley, who must have liked it. Then she said, "What? A group of three? Oh, I see what you mean. All right. I'll think about it. You call Charlotte, then call me back, okay?"

Vanessa hung up. She returned to the rec room, where Mallory was giving the triplets a hand with their haunted house. (Jessi had gone outdoors to help Claire, Margo, and Nicky.)

"Haley says that cheerleaders should dress alike," Vanessa reported to Mal. "So we have to be the Three Somethings, only we don't know what."

"How about the Three Little Kittens?" suggested Adam, snickering.

"Or the Three Little Pigs?" said Jordan.

"No!" cried Vanessa.

"They're just teasing you," Mal told her gently.

The phone rang then, and Vanessa dashed for it, crying, "That's probably Haley! I bet she and Charlotte have a good idea for our costumes."

"Big deal," muttered Adam.

A few moments later, Vanessa reappeared. "Charlotte and Haley are coming over."

"Goody," said Jordan. "Just what we need. More girls."

"Enough," Mallory told him warningly.

The cheerleaders holed up in the bedroom that Mal and Vanessa share. They talked for almost an hour about costumes. At last they ran down to the rec room, looking very excited.

"We know what we're going to be! We know what we're going to be!" cried Charlotte, who doesn't usually get very noisy.

"What?" asked Mal, quite interested.

The girls looked at each other and grinned. Then they said in unison, "The Three . . . Stooges!"

Mal tried (successfully) not to laugh. "The Three Stooges?" she repeated.

"Yup," said Haley.

"*And*," added Vanessa, "we're going to go trick-or-treating together. The Three Stooges costumes will be for Halloween, too. Now I don't have to worry about what a poetess looks like."

"Boy," said Adam enviously. "*We* should have thought of that. The Three Stooges would be perfect costumes for triplets."

"You can be The Three Stooges, too, if you want," said Vanessa generously.

"No way!" exclaimed Jordan. "Not if the idea is already taken by *girls*."

The girls ignored Jordan's comment. They found the *TV Guide* and began looking through it to see if any Three Stooges programs were going to be on soon. They wanted to copy the costumes of Larry, Moe, and Curly. The triplets returned to their spook-house preparations.

In the backyard, Nicky yelled, "Home run! All *right!*"

The afternoon was, Mal and Jessi agreed, a fun one.

CHAPTER 8

At first, I couldn't figure out why my friends were looking so astonished. Finally Mary Anne stood up and whispered in my ear, "The *clock*, Kristy."

It was Monday afternoon. The seven BSC members were gathered in Claud's bedroom. As usual, I was sitting in the director's chair, visor in place, pencil over one ear. What had astonished everybody was that the clock had changed from 5:29 to 5:30 and then to 5:31 — and I had not said a word. I had not called the meeting to order. I was just sitting in the chair, staring into space.

"Oh. Oh, um. Order, everybody," I said hastily. I paused.

"Kristy, are you all right?" asked Stacey.

"Yeah. I just forgot to start the meeting, that's all."

"You forgot to tell me to collect dues, too," said Stacey. "It *is* Monday. And what do you mean you forgot to start the meeting?"

"Oh, nothing. . . . Stacey, it's dues day."

"No kidding." Stacey made us fork over. Then my friends just gaped at me.

"What?" I said.

"Well, what is *wrong*?" asked Mary Anne. "You've never sat by the clock and not noticed when it said five-thirty."

"Yeah. Maybe you shouldn't be president after all," teased Dawn.

I tried to laugh, but it wasn't much of an effort.

"Kristy?" said Claud. "Come on. Get with it."

I sighed. "Okay. I was too embarrassed to tell you guys this, but I've gotten four more notes from the mystery admirer."

"So? You weren't embarrassed about the first fifty or so notes," said Stacey, smiling. I could tell she was trying to get me to smile, too.

"The last four notes," I began, "have been . . . weird."

Everyone immediately looked interested, and I could tell that we weren't going to have a normal meeting. ·

"What did the notes say?" Jessi wanted to know.

"Well, the first one wasn't *so* bad. Just kind

of odd," I replied. "It said, 'I love you, I love you, I love you. But beware. Love is fickle and so are friends.' Or something like that. Then the second note said, 'Violets are blue, blood is red, I'll remember you when you are dead.' "

"*What?*" screeched all my friends.

"Yup. That's *exactly* what that note said. I'll never forget it. Then the third note was about, let's see, blood again, but I didn't memorize that one. And anyway, today, just before Charlie drove me to the meeting, I got this note."

I pulled a piece of paper out of my pocket. My friends jumped up and leaned over me, peering at the note. They surrounded my chair, and I felt smothered.

"Ew," said Stacey. She took the paper from me and read aloud. "I want to be with you forever — eternal togetherness. So I am coming to get you."

"Aughh!" shrieked Mary Anne. "He's coming to *get* you?"

"*Now* are you guys so sure the notes are from Bart?" I asked.

"No," replied everyone else.

"They must be from Sam," added Claudia.

"That's what I said in the first place and no one listened to me!" I cried. "Now that the notes are weird, you think they're from my brother after all. But even Sam wouldn't go this far. I know him and his jokes too well. He'd stop after about two notes and find some way to let me know he was behind them. Sam likes to take credit for his work and he can't wait very long for it."

"Well, who *are* the notes from then?" Mal wondered. (Everyone was settling back into their places.) "They can't be from Bart."

"I'm not so sure," I replied. "Maybe he's, like, really sick or something. I read this book once about a fourteen-year-old boy everyone thought was so normal and nice, and it turned out he was . . . a cold-blooded killer."

"Kristy!" exclaimed Stacey. (She sounded like my mother.)

"Well, that's what the book was about."

"Was it a true story?" asked Stacey.

"No," I answered. "But it could have been."

Stacey looked as if she were about to say, "See?"

"Before you say anything," I rushed on, "remember the notes. They're real. *Someone* is sending them."

The room was quiet. No one knew what to say. I felt that I had to remind my friends about one small point.

"I invited Bart to the Halloween Hop, don't forget," I said.

"Aughh!" shrieked Mary Anne again. "You're going with a psycho!"

"Oh, my lord," whispered Claudia.

"Now just a second," said Mallory calmly, "you *don't* know that the notes are from Bart."

"I don't know that they *aren't* from Bart, either," I pointed out, "and I don't want to take any chances."

"What are you saying?" asked Dawn.

"I'm thinking of un-inviting Bart to the Hop."

"Oh, Kristy!" exclaimed Stacey.

But the phone rang before she could go on. (I'd almost forgotten that we were having a club meeting.)

We took the calls that came in for the next few minutes, lining up jobs with the Rodowsky boys, the Kuhns, the Perkinses, and Jenny Prezzioso.

Then Stacey immediately said, "Kristy, you can't un-invite Bart to the dance, especially when you don't even know if the notes are from him. I think you should confront him. Ask him straight out if he's your mystery admirer, and if he is, why he would write such awful things." She shivered. "I can't help thinking about that 'I'll remember you when you are dead' poem. That gave me the creeps."

"Think how *I* feel!" I said. "And anyway, I don't know about confronting him. Would *you* confront a psycho?"

"You don't know for sure if he *is* the psycho. I mean, *a* psycho," said Jessi. "I believe in giving a person the benefit of — "

"Wait a second!" I cried. "Oh, no! Oh, *no!* I just thought of something. You made me think of it, Jessi. You said, 'A psycho.' "

"So?" said Jessi, and the rest of my friends looked puzzled.

"What," I began, "if the notes aren't from Bart or Sam or anyone else we can think of? What if they *are* from just 'a psycho'?"

"Well — " Stacey started to say.

But I kept right on going. "Don't forget. I'm rich. I mean, I'm Watson Brewer's stepdaughter, and Watson is a millionaire. What if some weirdo out there is playing a cat-and-mouse game and then, when he's ready, he's going to pounce on me?"

My friends looked more puzzled than ever.

"*Kid*nap me," I explained. "He's going to scare me to death, then kidnap me and ask Watson for the ransom money. Watson could afford to pay the ransom, and he'd do it. I'm sure he would."

"You know," said Mal, "we just read this short story in English class. It was by an author named O. Henry, and it was called 'The Ransom of Red Chief.' In it, these guys kidnap this little boy, only it turns out that the boy is such an awful child his parents don't want him back, so they refuse to pay the ransom and the kidnappers are stuck with the boy."

Jessi, Dawn, and Mary Anne snickered. Claud and Stacey managed not to snicker, but even they couldn't keep from smiling.

"Come on, you guys. This is serious," I said. "I *have* been getting notes, Watson *is* rich, and things like this *do* happen — and not just on TV, either. They happen in real life. Where do you think the TV writers get their ideas from?"

That shut everyone up and stopped the smiling.

But then Stacey, our skeptic, said, "Oh, Kristy, this really *is* ridiculous. No one's going to kidnap you."

"Convince me," I said.

My fellow BSC members looked everywhere but at me.

"The notes said he was coming to get me," I reminded my friends.

"*One* note said that," Mary Anne pointed out. "*One* note."

"I'm not convinced," was my only reply.

Later that night, I sat in my room and tried to do my homework. Needless to say, I could not concentrate. I couldn't think of my room as just a room. It had become a room in a *mansion*. And Watson wasn't just my step-father, he was a *millionaire*.

I abandoned my homework. I got up from my desk, took all the notes out of their hiding place between the pages of *The Cat Ate My Gymsuit*, and spread the notes on my bed in the order in which I'd received them. I read them. I looked at them. I examined the paper, the typing, the stickers, the envelopes.

They were definitely the work of a lunatic. *But he was not going to get me.*

I jumped up. I ran from window to window in my room and made sure they were shut and locked. I checked the lock on my door. It worked, too. Mom and Watson tell my broth-ers and sisters and me not to lock our doors at night because it's a fire hazard, but I would have to risk that. I figured there was a better chance of getting kidnapped than of Watson's house (excuse me, his mansion) burning down. Why did Mom have to marry a rich guy?

Then I thought of something horrible. A lunatic could get into my room through one of the windows even if it was locked. He'd simply wrap some cloth around his hand, punch through a pane of glass, reach in and unlock the window from the inside, and open it. Of course, I'm on the second floor, but the kidnapper could climb a ladder. He could be quiet. And in the dead of night, who would notice him?

I was trying to figure out how to board up my windows when something else occurred to me: The kidnapper could get me *any* time. He could get me walking to my house from the bus stop or on my way into school or to a baby-sitting job. I decided that I should try to be with people as much as possible. It would be harder to kidnap me if I weren't alone.

Should I tell Mom and Watson about the danger I was in? I wondered. No. They might think I was crazy.

I turned on my radio. I needed to listen to reports of missing lunatics. As far as I knew, there were no insane asylums around Stoneybrook, but who knows what a psycho is capable of?

I tuned in just in time for the news. I heard about the President's press conference, a plane crash, a kid who was raising money to help fight drug abuse by running all the way from Connecticut to New York City, and I heard the sports and weather reports.

But the newscaster didn't say a word about a missing lunatic.

Okay, so he wasn't escaped. He was a *new* lunatic, one who hadn't been caught yet.

I didn't finish my homework that night.

CHAPTER 9

Two days later I told Shannon my lunatic theory. She thought *I* was a lunatic for having come up with it. In fact, she had a new theory.

"I think," said Shannon, who had either read or heard about every single note I'd received, "that Bart is the note writer."

"But you said he couldn't be. You said you go to school with him and you know him and — "

"I know what I said, but listen. I think Bart's afraid your Krushers are going to beat his Bashers in the World Series, so he's trying to psyche you out. He's trying to make you crazy so you won't be a good coach and the Krushers will play badly and lose."

I was incensed. Especially considering that Shannon and I were on our way to the ball field for a game against the Bashers. (As we walked along, I kept my eye out for slow-driving, suspicious-looking cars.)

Ahead of us were walking David Michael, the Papadakis kids, and a couple of other Krushers from our neighborhood. They were laughing and talking, paying no attention to Shannon and me.

"Well, if that's what Bart is doing, that is really . . . that is really *despicable!*" I exclaimed. (That was the worst thing I could think of to say.)

"I know," said Shannon. "I agree. I refused to speak to him in school today."

"Thank you," I told her.

The thought that the notes might be from Bart after all did two things for me. One, it made me less worried about a lunatic being after me, and two, it made me incredibly angry — which was good. The more angry I am the more energy I have, and the more energy I have, the better I coach the Krushers. We were going to beat the Bashers that day.

"You know what else is wrong with your lunatic theory?" asked Shannon as we reached the playing field.

"What?" I replied, even though I was tired of hearing about all the things wrong with my theory.

"If a psycho really did want ransom money, why wouldn't he kidnap Karen or Andrew?

They're Watson's own children, plus they're littler and they'd be easier to capture."

I just made a face. I didn't like the way Shannon had implied that "real" children are more important than stepchildren. And I didn't like to think about Karen or Andrew being kidnapped.

Shannon didn't see my face, though. She had spotted Mary Anne and Dawn. They were sitting under a tree. Dawn had brought the Braddock kids to the ball field (Matt as a player, Haley as a cheerleader), and Mary Anne had just come along to cheer the Krushers on. Shannon ran over to them and they began to talk. I almost joined them, but I was a little angry at Shannon for making those comments (even though I knew she hadn't meant to hurt me or upset me). Besides, the Krushers were excited and ready to begin the game, and the Bashers were nearby, looking tough.

I caught Bart's eye (he was surrounded by his team) and he grinned at me, but I just looked away. How could he smile at me like that?

The game began. The Krushers were up at bat first, and I'd placed Matt Braddock in the number-one spot in the lineup. He may be deaf, but he is one of our best hitters.

The Bashers pitcher wound up and slammed a ball to Matt.

CRACK!

Matt hit the ball with such force that I thought it would break a window at Stoneybrook Elementary. But it hit the ground first. An outfielder scrambled after it. Meanwhile, Matt was running bases and had lost sight of the ball. He hesitated at third base.

Nicky Pike signed something to him frantically and Matt frowned. He stayed where he was, looking completely confused. A few seconds later, the third baseman was holding the ball triumphantly, and Haley Braddock had her head in her hands.

"What's wrong?" I asked her.

"Nicky was signing, 'Swim! Swim!' to Matt. I think he meant to sign, 'Run, run.' Matt could have made a home run, but he didn't know what was going on."

No wonder Matt had looked confused, I thought. Then I said to Haley, "Will you explain things to Matt later? Tell him it wasn't his fault and I'm not mad. I'll talk to Nicky. I think he needs a refresher course in sign language from you, Haley."

Next up at bat was Claire Pike. She is not a good hitter, and I wanted to get her turn out of the way as quickly as possible. Claire surprised me, though. I think she surprised herself, too, when her bat connected with the first ball pitched and sailed away from her.

She hesitated for a fraction of a second, then took off for first base.

But — *SWOCK!* The pitcher caught Claire's ball on the fly.

"One out!" called the referee.

Claire immediately threw a tantrum. "Nofe-air! Nofe-air!"

I let Nicky and Vanessa calm her down and sent Jake Kuhn up to bat. He struck out. Two outs. Matt stood on third base with his hand on his hip, looking disgusted and disappointed. I couldn't blame him.

Jackie Rodowsky was up next. He swung and missed twice before getting a hit. But it was a low grounder, and the pitcher scooped the ball up and tossed it to the catcher, who got it just before Matt slid home. Three outs.

Matt looked like he was ready to kill someone, or maybe a lot of someones. First his chance at a home run had been ruined, then his chance to score.

"Don't worry," I said calmly to my team before they headed, discouraged, to the field. "The score is still zero to zero. Nicky, you're pitching. See if you can keep the game scoreless. The rest of you, just play your best."

Nicky did not, unfortunately, manage to keep the game scoreless. By the end of the first inning, the score was 3–0, in favor of the Bashers.

"Come on, you guys," I said cheerfully to the Krushers as the teams changed places again. "I know you can earn some runs this time. I can *feel* it. Now get out there and give it your best."

"Okay, Kristy Thomas," said Gabbie Perkins.

(I am always amazed at how the Krushers just keep on going. Sometimes they are disappointed or Claire throws a tantrum, but for the most part, the kids cheer each other on, don't begrudge anybody anything, and are understanding of each other and their shortcomings. Still, they must have been upset at the prospect of losing to the Bashers, after finally beating them, especially with the World Series just around the corner.)

The Krushers dutifully got into the batting order, though, and Buddy Barrett stepped up to the plate. He was nervous but trying not to show it.

The Basher pitcher wound up and let fly a fastball.

Buddy was prepared. *THWACK.* The ball

sailed through the air — but it was out of bounds.

And it hit Shannon on the head.

"OW!" she shrieked.

She and Dawn and Mary Anne had seen the ball coming toward them and, in trying to duck, had gotten in each other's way. Shannon hadn't been able to avoid the ball.

"I'm sorry! I'm sorry!" Dawn and Mary Anne cried.

"I'm sorrier!" That was Buddy. He and I and a whole group of kids had run over to Shannon.

"Are you all right?" everyone kept asking.

"I think so," Shannon replied, patting her head cautiously. (This is why we play *soft*ball.)

"Are you *really* all right?" asked Buddy anxiously.

"Yes, I really am." Shannon smiled at Buddy, and he looked back at her with what can only be called love.

Bart had run over to us by this time, along with some of his teammates.

"Are you okay, Shannon?" he asked, genuinely concerned. (Shannon was rubbing her head, even though she was smiling at Buddy.)

Shannon did not answer Bart. She didn't even look at him. (Neither did Mary Anne nor Dawn. I had a feeling Shannon had told them her suspicions about Bart.) And I focused on Shannon, feeling only mildly sorry for Bart.

When Shannon had convinced us that she truly was fine (or was going to be) and had even asked to keep the ball with which she'd been hit, the collected Krushers and Bashers finally returned to their game. Buddy lingered for a moment, though, received another smile from Shannon, then ran to catch up with his team.

The rest of the game went about the same way as the first inning. The Krushers simply were not a match for the Bashers that day, no matter how hard they tried, and no matter how loudly the cheerleaders shouted. In the end, the Bashers beat the Krushers 10–1, and that one run was suspect, but the Bashers "gave" it to us, since they already had eight runs at the time and the game was nearing its end.

When the game was over, Bart trotted up to me and said, "Good game, Kristy. You coached your kids well."

I glared at him. How could he try to psyche me out, then be so nice to me? Bart looked confused, but I pretended not to notice, and when he asked if he could walk me home, I thanked him but said I was busy. Then I joined Shannon, Dawn, and Mary Anne.

They were talking about Bart and the letters.

"Maybe," Dawn began, "he's not trying to psyche you out for the World Series. Maybe he's mad at you because of that fight you two had over how the series should be played. The weird letters started after the fight, didn't they?"

I nodded.

"And you know how boys hold grudges," said Shannon, sounding wise.

I shrugged. "Either way, what he's doing is crummy."

My friends agreed.

Then I had to leave. I had to help the Krushers with their equipment, see that everyone got picked up, and finally help Charlie load our car. He drove Karen, Andrew, David Michael, and me home, and I tried not to feel too depressed.

What had I gotten myself into? I was still supposed to go to the Halloween Hop with Bart, and Bart was either crazy or mean. (If he was the note writer. If he wasn't, I didn't want to think about who was.) Anyway, I had to decide whether to un-invite Bart to the dance.

Later, I was in the middle of figuring out how to do that, not having had much experience with boys, when our phone rang. Of course, it was Bart. Great.

I didn't even bother to sneak into the closet with the cordless phone. I just took the receiver from Mom, who had answered the extension in the kitchen and said, "Hi, Bart. I'm sorry but I can't talk to you now," and hung up.

As I returned the receiver to the cradle, I could hear him saying, "Hey, Kristy," but I didn't feel too bad. Not when I thought about his notes.

However, it took me a long time to fall asleep that night.

CHAPTER 10

Tuesday

This afternoon, I baby-sat for Buddy, Suzi, and Marnie Barrett. Since the World Series is coming up, it was off to the playing fields for a Krushers practice. Buddy and Suzi were really excited, especially since they had gotten a tiny Krushers T-shirt for their little sister to wear. I put it over Marnie's sweater, (the weather was too cool for just a T-shirt,) sat her in her stroller, and we were off.

87

Guess what. Buddy confessed that he has a crush on Shannon! Suzi teased him about that -- but only until he threatened to tell on something she'd done. Apparently, Suzi has committed some sort of household crime which only Buddy knows about, and he's holding it over her, using it to keep her in line, or else waiting for just the right moment to let it fly.

Anyway, Marnie was an angel during practice. She was very interested in Laura Perkins, who slept next to us in her stroller while Myriah and Gabbie played softball. (Claud was sitting for the Perkinses.) And the Krushers' poor practice didn't dampen Buddy's spirits because ... Shannon was there again!

When Mary Anne arrived at the Barretts', she found them organized, for once. Or maybe they're generally more organized now. Anyway, they were a far cry from the way Dawn Schafer used to find them when she first began sitting for them. The children were dressed and set for softball practice, Mrs. Barrett was ready to leave but wasn't in one of her mad dashes, their house was tidy, and Pow the dog had even been walked.

"Good-bye, you three," said Mrs. Barrett when she'd put on her coat. She kissed Buddy (who's eight), Suzi (who's five), and Marnie (who's two), wished Buddy and Suzi good luck at practice, and left.

"Well," said Mary Anne, "let's get going. We should leave now if you want to be at the ball field on time."

"Okay," said Buddy. He looked at Suzi. "Do you want to get it or should I?"

"I will!" Suzi cried.

Mary Anne had no idea what they were talking about, but she didn't have to wait long to find out. Suzi returned in a flash, holding something behind her back. She whipped it out and held it up proudly.

"It's a Krushers T-shirt for Marnie!" said Buddy.

"Yeah. She comes to almost all the games. She *needs* one," added Suzi.

So Mary Anne, smiling, put the shirt on over Marnie's sweater, checked to make sure everyone was wearing a hat, and led the kids out the back door to the garage, where Marnie's stroller was kept.

They set off, Buddy and Suzi chattering away, and Marnie pointing at things and crying out, "Doggie! *Big* doggie!" and, "Smell flowers, Mary Anne," and, "Play ball!" which made everyone laugh, because she had said it just like a sportscaster.

Then they fell into a silence, which was broken by Buddy saying tentatively, "I wonder if that girl will be there again."

"What girl?" asked Mary Anne.

"He means *Shan-non*," Suzi answered in a singsong voice.

Buddy blushed. "I hit her on the head at our last game and she wanted to keep the ball, just like a real fan."

"*Oh*," said Mary Anne, remembering.

"*Buddy li-ikes Shannon, Buddy li-ikes Shan-non*," sang Suzi.

"Want to make something of it?" asked Buddy, not denying the charge.

"*Buddy and Shannon, sitting in a tree —* " Suzi began.

Buddy grabbed her arm. "Cut it out!" he yelled. "Or I'll tell Mary Anne *and* Mom about the . . . you know."

Suzi was instantly quiet.

The rest of the walk to the ball field was quiet, but Mary Anne had a feeling that everyone (except Marnie) was thinking about or wondering about whatever Suzi had done. Mary Anne felt it wasn't her business to pry, though.

At the playing field, everyone oohed and ahhed — first over Marnie in her T-shirt, and then over the cheerleaders. They had gotten their costumes together and were wearing them. They had even managed to find wigs that matched The Three Stooges' hair.

A few kids laughed, but Charlotte, Vanessa, and Haley didn't care. Their costumes were funny and they knew it.

"*We* ought to pep you guys up," said Haley to the Krushers, and the Krushers agreed.

Everyone was in a good mood. I sensed that as soon as I set foot on the grounds of Stoneybrook Elementary. David Michael was with me. He had been talking nonstop about the World Series, which was fast approaching. Then there were Vanessa, Haley, and Charlotte in their crazy outfits, and Marnie Barrett in her little Krushers T-shirt.

I was probably the only one who wasn't entirely psyched for the game. I still didn't know what to do about Bart and the dance, and then, when I was leaving the house for practice, I found another note on our front steps. Thank goodness David Michael was still inside, looking for his mitt. I didn't want him to see what I'd found.

The new note said, "Beware. I'm coming sooner than you think. And once I find you, this is all that will be left of Kristin Amanda Thomas." I looked in the envelope and saw . . . fingernail clippings.

Oh, *ew. EW.* I almost dumped them out, but decided I might need them for evidence sometime.

"Hey, Kristy!" called David Michael then, and I thrust the envelope in the back pocket of my jeans.

"What?" I yelled back.

"I can't find my mitt."

So we had to have a mitt-search before we could leave for the ball field.

By the time we reached Stoneybrook Elementary, I was tired. David Michael and I had a fair amount of equipment to carry and no one to help us, although Charlie had said he'd pick me up after practice. So we had to carry everything ourselves. Besides being tired, my mind wasn't on the game. It was on Bart, the school dance, and the notes, especially the one I'd just received. So, despite The Three Stooges cheerleaders, practice did not go very well. But it was not entirely my fault.

Even though my Krushers were their usual enthusiastic selves, they just did not play well. Jackie Rodowsky kept tripping when he ran bases. Jamie Newton began ducking balls again. David Michael's pitching was not up to par.

I gathered the Krushers together after two innings of mistakes. "You guys," I said, "remember the basics, okay? All the old stuff. Pay attention to what you're doing. Keep your eye on the ball. Don't swing at wild pitches. And no fancy stuff. Concentrate on the game, not on stealing bases, okay?"

"O-kay!" chanted the Krushers.

"Do you need a break before we continue our game?"

"Maybe just a little one," replied Myriah.

"All right," I said. "Take ten."

I walked over to the trees, where Mary Anne and Claudia were sitting with Marnie Barrett, Laura Perkins . . . and Shannon!

"Hi, you guys," I said wearily, and then added, to Shannon, "When did you get here? I thought you were busy this afternoon."

"Our hockey practice was canceled," she replied.

"Well, I'm glad you came to watch us," I told her.

"Me, too," said a voice from behind me.

It was Buddy Barrett, gazing adoringly at Shannon. (I had no idea what was going on then, because I hadn't read Mary Anne's notebook entry yet.)

"Hey, Buddy," I said, "could you go give Jackie some hitting tips?"

"Sure," he replied, looking both pleased and disappointed. (Disappointed at not being able to stay with Shannon, I guess.)

"Is anything wrong?" Mary Anne asked me.

I nodded. "Yeah. This." I pulled the envelope out of my pocket and showed my friends the newest note.

Their reaction was nearly the same as mine had been:

"Gross!" (Claudia)

"Repulsive!" (Mary Anne)

"Disgusting!" (Shannon)

After that, no one knew what to say, but I had a feeling we were all wondering the same thing. Would Bart *really* do something so gross, repulsive, and disgusting?

"Well," I said, "back to the game. Cheer us on, you guys."

The Krushers returned to their practice. The third inning began. And on David Michael's first pitch, Buddy Barrett swung and hit the ball with a loud *crack!* I saw Mary Anne and Claudia throw themselves in front of the strollers, and Shannon duck and cover her head. But they didn't need to worry. The ball sailed into the outfield. Buddy had hit a double.

"Yea!" cheered Shannon.

And that was the end of our good luck. Jake Kuhn fouled out. David Michael's pitching went downhill. Then Jackie hit a double himself, but tripped and fell just as he was approaching second base.

"Out!" yelled Nicky Pike.

At least Buddy made it home, scoring one run.

The cheerleaders went wild. "Who are the greatest? Who are the greatest?" they yelled, jumping up and down. "The Krushers, the Krushers! Yea!"

By the time they were finished, all of their wigs had fallen off, and Vanessa's pants were practically at her knees.

"Vanessa!" hissed Haley, aghast.

"I know, I know." Vanessa tugged desperately at her pants.

"I guess we'll have to work a little harder on our costumes," said Charlotte.

After another inning, I called a halt to practice. Nothing was being accomplished. Margo Pike was in the outfield, blowing on blades of grass and staring into space. David Michael was paying more attention to a scrape on his elbow than to his pitching. Buddy had eyes only for Shannon, and even I wasn't concentrating. Not on the game, anyway, but I sure couldn't keep my mind off the notes.

Mary Anne rounded up Buddy and Suzi and set off for the Barretts'. Their mother would be home soon. Suzi seemed gloomy as they walked along, but Buddy was in seventh heaven.

"Did you hear how Shannon cheered for me?" he asked.

"Buddy and Shannon, sitting in a tree — " sang Suzi.

"Suzi, one more word and I'll tell about the . . ."

"Okay, okay, okay."

Mary Anne smiled — then remembered the fingernail clippings and stopped her smiling abruptly.

CHAPTER 11

After our disastrous practice, Bart once again appeared at the schoolyard and asked to walk me home. And once again, I rode with Charlie instead.

"What's *with* you?" Bart called after me as I climbed into the car. "Why won't you *speak* to me? Why won't *Shannon* speak to me? Girls are . . ."

His voice faded away as we drove off.

"Why *won't* you speak to Bart?" Charlie wanted to know, glancing at me in the rearview mirror and frowning.

But I wouldn't answer him, either.

And that night, when Bart called, I said to Sam, "Tell him I've gone to Europe," which Sam did with a certain amount of glee. Telling Bart I'd gone to Europe was tantamount to a goof call, for Sam.

* * *

Considering all this, you can imagine how surprised I was when the doorbell rang the next afternoon, and who should I find on our front steps but Bart.

"Bart!" I exclaimed.

"Can I come in?" he asked seriously.

"I guess so," I replied. Nannie was home. Sam, too. I wasn't baby-sitting, and it's a lot easier to hang up on somebody (or have your brother tell him you've gone to Europe) than it is to slam a door in his face.

Bart stepped inside and I closed the door behind him. "We have to talk," he said. "In private. Where can we go?"

"My room, I guess," I answered with a sigh. I went to the kitchen, told Nannie that Bart was here and we were going to my room to talk, then led him upstairs. This felt weird. Bart had only been inside my house a few times, and he had certainly never been inside my room. I fervently hoped that I hadn't left any underwear lying around and that my room was at least reasonably neat. (I'm not exactly a slob, but if anybody were ever asked to list ten things that describe me, the word *neat* would not come to mind.)

I walked into my room ahead of Bart and was relieved to see that it was presentable.

(There might have been some underwear under the bed, but Bart would never know.) I looked around to see who should sit where, and decided that I should sit in my desk chair and Bart should get the armchair.

"So?" he said, trying to fold his tall body into the small chair.

"So?" I countered.

"Kristy, what . . . is . . . going . . . on?" he said in a measured voice.

"I think you know."

"I do not. If I knew, I wouldn't be here right now."

"You sure are a good liar," I said bluntly.

"*Liar?!* I'm not lying. I don't know what's going on and I want you to tell me. Either you or Shannon. But you're the one I'm supposed to be going to a dance with," said Bart. He looked angry and I began to feel afraid. First of all, I'd never seen him this angry. Second, it probably wasn't a good idea to get a lunatic angry. I was glad that Nannie and Sam were home.

But I didn't let Bart see my fear. "Okay. You want to know what's going on? I'll show you what's going on." I marched over to my bookshelf, pulled out *The Cat Ate My Gymsuit*, and removed the notes from between the pages.

Then I spread them across the bed. "There. That's what's going on — as if you didn't know."

Bart looked at the first few notes — the love letters — and reddened.

"So you did write them," I said.

"Yeah," admitted Bart. "Only I didn't write this many." He frowned and read the rest of the notes. When he was finished, he looked at me with horror. "You think *I* wrote these notes to you?" He peeked into the envelope containing the fingernail clippings. "You think I *sent* these to you? How could you think that? And *why* would I do this?"

"I — I don't — " I stumbled over my words. "To psyche me out so the Krushers would lose the World Series?" I suggested feebly.

"That's crazy!" Bart was almost shouting.

"SHHH!" I hissed.

"Well, it is crazy," said Bart, lowering his voice. "It's the craziest thing I can think of. If we play, we play fair and square." He paused. Then he asked, "Does Shannon know about these letters? Is that why she hasn't been speaking to me?"

I nodded. (I thought Bart would explode.) "Well, you did send some of the letters," I pointed out.

"Yeah, the — the, um — the *nice* ones," agreed Bart. I was melting. Bart *really liked* me. But he was still angry.

"Listen," I said, "I'm sorry for accusing you of sending the notes, especially in order to psyche me out," (I didn't mention that that had been Shannon's idea), "but it was easier to believe that than to believe . . ."

"To believe what?" asked Bart curiously.

"That some lunatic was sending them. I'm afraid someone's going to kidnap me and ask Watson for the ransom money. I mean, the guy does say he's going to get me. And then he keeps talking about death."

Bart sighed. "I can see why you'd be scared," he said, "but I still can't believe that *you* would believe that *I* would . . . oh, forget it."

For a few seconds Bart and I just looked at each other. I felt so confused. Finally I said quietly, "Thank you for the first notes. I liked them a lot. That's why I saved them."

"Really?" said Bart.

"Yeah. I did. I never got" (I almost said *love letters*) "I never got notes like those before. I felt . . . I don't know how I felt. But I know I'll never throw those letters away."

Bart smiled. "That's how I wanted you to

feel. You're really special, Kristy." (I know I blushed.) Then he asked, "What about the other letters?"

"Why did I keep them, too?"

"No, I mean *what about* them? Where did they come from? Who sent them? What do they mean?"

I was relaxing. Even though I didn't have the answers to Bart's questions, I felt as if things were falling into place. Bart had written the love letters. That made sense. Then someone else had written the scary letters.

"I don't know," I told Bart. "Shannon and I have read the letters a million times and we can't come up with a thing."

Bart leaned over. Just as I had done so often, he read all the horrible letters to himself again. He even murmured the poem aloud, shivering at the "I'll remember you when you are dead" part.

"See why I'm afraid they're from a lunatic?" I said.

"Well, I can see why they frighten you, but a *lu*natic? I don't know, Kristy. That sounds like — "

"Don't say, 'That sounds like something you'd see on TV.' "

"Okay, I won't. . . . But it does."

I sighed. "I know. Still, I don't have any better ideas."

"Got any enemies?" asked Bart.

I shook my head slowly. "I don't think so. Not unless you count Alan Gray, but he's too much of a dweeb to think up something like this."

"Who's Alan Gray?"

"A jerk. A boy at school who's been a pest all his life and probably will remain that way into adulthood."

Bart laughed. "But he wouldn't do this?" He pointed to the letters.

"No. I don't think so. It takes brains to do that."

"What about Sam?"

It was my turn to laugh. "Poor Sam," I said. "Everyone fingers him as a likely suspect. He's going to have trouble living down his reputation. Shannon thought the notes were from Sam, my friends at school thought they were from him. Even *I* thought the first ones were from him, before I could believe that any boy would like me enough to send me lo — to send me notes like those," I said.

"Hmm," said Bart, looking deep in thought. "Kristy, how many people know about the notes?"

"Well, let's see. Just Shannon, my friends in the Baby-sitters Club, and now you. Oh, and David Michael was here when Shannon brought the first letter over. It was in her mailbox for some reason."

"Oh," said Bart. "That was Kyle's fault, I guess. He must have gotten the mailboxes mixed up. I, um, I sent him to deliver the notes. I was afraid to go myself. I thought someone might see me on your street and you'd figure out who was sending the notes."

I giggled. "You don't have to explain anything to me."

"So," Bart went on, "pretty many people know you've been getting notes."

"I guess so," I replied. "But what — ?" I was interrupted by David Michael yelling up the stairs. "Kristy? Phone for you!"

"Just a sec," I said to Bart. I answered the second-floor extension. It was Shannon. I told her what was going on and invited her over. I figured that with three people, we could do some real brainstorming.

So Shannon came over. After she apologized to Bart for having given him the silent treatment, she sat on my bed, being careful not to disturb the notes. "Any theories about the notes?" she asked us, sounding like a detective.

"No theories," I answered. "But we know there are two people responsible for them. Bart did write the first notes, the nice ones, just like you thought. But somebody *else* is writing the others. The question is *who?* And don't say Sam," I said quickly.

"Kristy doesn't have any enemies," Bart added.

"Maybe someone *is* trying to sabotage the Krushers and make them lose the World Series. Can either of you think of anybody who would want to win so badly that they'd do all this?" Shannon waved her hand across the bed, indicating the notes.

Bart and I shook our heads, and Bart added, "None of the Bashers is old enough to do something like that. And I'm sure none of their parents would do it." He paused. "You know what's weird, though? The scary notes look just like the ones *I* wrote. Who could have seen me writing the notes? I did that privately."

Neither Shannon nor I had any suggestions. Kyle was too little to think up awful letters, and Bart doesn't have any other brothers or sisters.

"It's got to be a crazy person, then," I said. "There's no other answer. He'd been watching our house, he saw Kyle delivering the notes, and he opened a couple before I did. You didn't always seal them," I said to Bart. "Sometimes you just stuck the flap down with a sticker. The stickers peeled off easily." I put my head in my hands. "Oh," I moaned, "there really is a kidnapper after me."

"I still think that's farfetched," said Bart firmly. "There's another answer. I just don't know what it is."

"Me neither," said Shannon.

"Me neither," I said.

I went to bed that night thinking only of being kidnapped. Every creak or rustle in our old house made me jump. A car honked and I nearly fell out of bed. It took me forever to drift off to sleep . . . after I thought I'd seen a face at my window.

CHAPTER 12

On Saturday, a week before Halloween, and six days before Bart and I would go to the Halloween Hop, I woke up without a pit in my stomach for once; without a worry about being kidnapped.

It was the day of the World Series and I could think of nothing but softball and the game that was to be played. It was going to be a big event. Both the Krushers and the Bashers had been practicing hard and were geared up for the game. Parents and brothers and sisters would be sitting in the bleachers. So would friends, and of course, the members of the BSC. And The Three Stooges would be present to cheer the Krushers on.

There was an awful lot of excitement at my house that morning. Karen and Andrew were not spending the weekend with us, but they had come over early, and both they and David Michael (all Krushers) were racing around in a state of . . . I'm not sure what. They were certainly keyed up.

"Our T-shirts have to be clean!" I could hear Karen say as I put on my robe and went downstairs for breakfast.

"And we have to bulk up," added David Michael, whom I found seated in front of an enormous bowl of cereal and a stack of toast. "I need starch," he was telling Mom matter-of-factly. "So do you," he added to Karen and Andrew.

"I can't eat all that!" exclaimed Andrew. "Besides, I already ate breakfast."

"You guys, calm down," I said. They were practically bouncing off the walls, just like they'd been on the morning of the first game we ever played against the Bashers. "Eat what you feel like eating," I said. Then I turned to Mom. "Is everything ready for the refreshment stand?" I asked her. (We were going to have a Krushers refreshment stand, just like we'd had at our first game against the Bashers. The parents had chipped in with cookies and lemonade to sell to the fans. We were trying to earn enough money for team baseball caps. We'd almost earned enough the last time, but then Jackie Rodowsky had managed to knock over the refreshment stand with a flying bat, so we'd lost a few things. In the end, we'd earned some money for our team, but not enough for hats for everyone. We were hoping we could accomplish that today.)

"Everything's set," replied Mom. "Sam and Charlie will bring the tables in the station wagon. Oh, and I made brownies for you to sell."

"You did?" I cried. "Thanks, Mom! You were only supposed to supply the tables. Boy, our refreshment stand is going to be great."

"Well," said Mom, "I figured you might need some extra food — in case your walking disaster has another disaster."

"Thanks," I said gratefully.

And then, just like before any big game, the phone calls started. Kids were nervous. Kids had lost their T-shirts. They'd forgotten tips that I'd given them. Jake Kuhn's younger sister was sick and wouldn't be able to play. I tried to remain calm, mostly for the sake of Karen, Andrew, and David Michael, who were, by then, at about an eleven on an excitement scale of one to ten.

Our game was set to begin at noon that day. But I needed to arrive earlier, so my family left at 10:45. We set out in two cars — everybody, every single person in my family from

Emily to Nannie. And we were loaded down with equipment, food, and the refreshment tables.

When we reached the grounds of Stoneybrook Elementary, we were the first ones there, but I knew that a crowd would gather quickly and soon the bleachers would be full.

I was right. By about twenty minutes after eleven, people were streaming onto the playing field. Charlie and Sam, who had volunteered to man the refreshment stand, were already doing business. The Krushers were gathering around me, anxious, and eyeing the Bashers as they appeared. The Bashers, as usual, were impressive. They're bigger than my Krushers, for the most part, and have T-shirts *and* baseball caps. (Matching, of course, which was what we were hoping to earn enough money for that day.) Then there are the Basher cheerleaders — four girls with actual cheerleaders' outfits — pleated skirts, the whole bit. The best that Vanessa, Haley, and Charlotte usually do are Krushers T-shirts, matching flared jean skirts, white knee socks, and sneakers. On the day of the World Series, though, they were The Three Stooges. Nobody knew quite what to make of them. At least they drew attention to themselves.

I hoped their wigs wouldn't fall off. Or their pants.

I was just about to give the Krushers a pep talk when, for some reason, I glanced up into the bleachers.

My eyes landed on Cokie and her friends!

What on earth were they doing at our World Series? None of them had brothers or sisters on either softball team, and they certainly were not friends of ours. As far as I was concerned their appearance at the game was suspicious. Why were they there? Were they going to make fun of the Krushers? Or *me?* I know I'm not as cool as they think *they* are, but that wasn't any reason to come ruin the game.

I almost went into the stands to talk to them, but then I thought better of it. My Krushers had surrounded me. They needed me. And if Cokie made any trouble, then my BSC friends would take care of them. I hoped.

"Okay, you guys," I said to the kids. "We've still got some time before the game. I'd like you to do some warm-ups. Nicky and David Michael, practice pitching to each other. Jake, you pitch some balls to these five," (I pulled a group of kids away from the others) "so they can practice hitting."

When all the kids were busy, I snagged

Mary Anne and pointed Cokie out to her. "What do you think she's doing here?"

Mary Anne shrugged. She wasn't nearly as suspicious as I was, despite what Cokie had done to her in the past. After a moment she said, "I think Cokie's just going to watch the game. Grace and the others, too."

"Oh, you know darn well that's not — "

"OW!"

Mary Anne and I were interrupted by a cry. Without even looking, I knew it had come from Jackie, the walking disaster. "Oh, brother," I muttered.

I turned around.

Jackie was rubbing his elbow, but he seemed all right.

I sighed. I hoped the Krushers were *really* ready for the World Series. They could beat the Bashers again if they tried hard enough. I knew they could. Their record was poor, but they could overcome it.

"What?" said Mary Anne. "Is anything wrong?"

I hesitated. "No," I said at last.

Mary Anne returned to Shannon and Logan and Claud and the rest of my friends. I searched for Bart and found him breaking up a fight between two of his toughest Bashers. When things had calmed down, we smiled at each other. Boy, was it hard to like a guy and want to cream his softball team at the same time.

"Hi," said Bart.

"Hi," I replied.

"Are you ready?" he asked.

"As we'll ever be. Are you?"

"I guess so. My team is all keyed up. They can't stop thinking about being beaten by the Krushers."

I couldn't help it. Inwardly, I gloated.

"So," I said, "same rules as before? A seven-inning game, Gabbie gets to hit a wiffle ball and stand closer to the pitcher, and we toss a coin to see which team goes to bat first?"

"Fine with me . . . Coach," replied Bart, smiling.

"Oh, and just remind your team that we have to sign to Matt Braddock."

"You got it."

Bart was off then, in answer to a kid who'd been pestering him for help with something for at least five minutes.

I turned around, all set to call the Krushers together for a pep talk — and ran right into Cokie.

"Hi, Kristy," she said a little too casually, if you know what I mean.

"Hi," I replied coolly.

"So how are things?"

"What things?" I replied

"You know. *Things*. Life."

"Fine."

"Is your team up for the game?"

"Cokie, what are you doing here?" I demanded.

"I just want to see the game."

"Why?"

"Oh, to show my support for your team."

I rolled my eyes. *"Why?"*

"Can't you accept it, Kristy? I'm not your enemy."

Well, she certainly wasn't my best friend.

"Anyway," Cokie went on, "I thought you might need a little extra cheering. You've looked sort of depressed lately. I want your team to win."

"I haven't been depressed!" I cried. "I've even got a boyfriend. He's coming to the Halloween Hop with me."

"Really?" said Cokie. "You must like each other a lot."

I drew myself up. I knew I was showing off, but I couldn't help saying, "We plan to spend our lives together."

I'd thought Cokie might screech, "You mean, you're getting *mar*ried?" Instead she said, "Aw. That's nice. Eternal togetherness?"

Cokie caught what she'd said before I did, and she blushed. That was when I remembered. "Eternal togetherness." That had been a phrase from one of the lunatic notes. "*You* wrote the scary letters!" I exclaimed.

It was too late. Cokie knew she'd given herself away. She couldn't even think of anything to say. She just began to back away from me. I may be short, but I'm strong and good at athletics. Every kid in my grade knows it.

"Just a second," I said through gritted teeth. I reached out and caught Cokie's sleeve. "You stay right here. I have some questions for you."

Cokie looked so afraid that I knew she'd answer anything I asked her — and answer truthfully.

"Did you send all those letters — all the frightening ones?" I demanded.

Cokie looked at the ground. "Yes." I still hadn't let go of her sleeve and she tried to squirm away, but I held on tightly.

"Why?"

"Because of . . . because of what you and your friends did to me and my friends in the graveyard. You made us look like fools in front of Logan."

"Too bad. You started the whole thing by trying to make Mary Anne look like a fool in front of Logan." Cokie didn't say anything, so I went on. "How did you know what to make the letters look like? They match Bart's perfectly. Stickers and everything."

"Well, you weren't too subtle about Bart's letters. You brought them to school and showed them to your friends at lunchtime. Practically the whole cafeteria saw those letters." Cokie made it sound like *her* letters were *my* fault.

I let go of her sleeve then. I was a jumble of feelings. First of all, I was relieved. There was no one after me. I didn't have to worry about being kidnapped anymore. Second, I was furious with Cokie. "By Monday," I said, "the whole school is going to know what you did. And maybe everyone at Stoneybrook Day School, too. Think about that. If you felt like a fool before, it won't be anything compared to now."

Cokie ran away. She snagged Grace, Lisa, and Bebe in the bleachers, and the four of them left in a hurry.

More than anything, what I wanted to do then was rush to my friends and tell them the news, but it was almost noon and time for the game. I found that I was filled with rage at Cokie, and therefore filled with energy, almost with exuberance.

116

I signaled to Bart. "Time to start the game," I told him, "and I've got news. I found out who the letter writer is and we don't have a thing to worry about. I'll tell you everything after the game."

Bart grinned. "Okay, Coach."

We gathered our teams and tossed a coin. The Krushers would be at bat first.

"Play ball!" shouted Bart.

CHAPTER 13

The game was off to a good start. I sent Matt Braddock out as our first batter, and he hit the first pitch with a resounding *whack*, running to third base before I signaled him to stop.

Next I sent Jake Kuhn to bat. He made it to first base and Matt made it home. One run for the Krushers! They were elated. They were also very involved with the game. Sometimes while they're waiting for their turn at bat, the little ones get fidgety and I have to recruit my friends to keep them occupied. Not during the World Series, though.

By the end of the first inning, the score was two to one, in favor of . . . the Krushers. The game was intense. I stood on the sidelines, chewing gum and paying attention to every little thing that happened. I remembered which kids needed what coaching tips when. I didn't let my team members try anything fancy. I shouted encouragement — but never scolded.

Bart began to look nervous.

During the second inning, although I thought it was a little risky, I let Gabbie Perkins, Claire Pike, and Jackie Rodowsky go to bat. Gabbie (with her special playing rules) hit a single, Claire struck out but did not throw a tantrum, and Jackie hit a home run! (He lost his balance, tripped, and fell as his teammates surrounded him to congratulate him, but I don't think the Bashers noticed. At any rate, nobody laughed at him.)

The Bashers, tough as nails, were now on their guard. There was no jeering at the Krushers as there had been during past games. They concentrated, playing a game that was as intense as I felt.

At one point during the third inning, with the Krushers still ahead (by one run), I glanced at Bart. He was looking at me rather fiercely. Oh, no, I thought. We just got over the nasty note business, and now we're going to go back to our old competitive selves. If the Krushers won today, would Bart still go to the dance with me? I wondered. I couldn't worry about that. I put the thought out of my head and whispered to David Michael, who was about to go up to bat, "Bunt it!"

When the score was six to five (still our favor!) we took a fifth-inning stretch. "You guys are doing a *great* job!" I told the Krushers. "Absolutely terrific. You're playing well, you're trying hard, and you're not letting the Bashers scare you."

The Krushers beamed.

I wandered over to the refreshment stand.

"You've easily got enough money for hats now," Sam told me. "People have been buying stuff all morning. And — and your team is playing, um, well." (It is not easy for Sam to be serious or to give compliments.)

"Thanks," I said gratefully, and bought a cup of lemonade. Then I sought out The Three Stooges. "I think you're a hit," I told them. (Their wigs and pants were still on.)

"Really?" exclaimed Charlotte from under a fringe of black bangs.

"Goody," added Haley.

I had to admit that the Bashers cheerleaders were more polished — but The Three Stooges attracted more attention.

Twenty minutes later, the game began again. And two innings later, it was over. The score was eight to seven.

The Krushers had won the World Series!

You should have seen the hugging and jumping up and down, and heard the whooping and cheering in the stands. The Krushers were beside themselves but had the presence of mind to join The Three Stooges in a cheer of, "Two, four, six, eight. Who do we appreciate? The Bashers! The Bashers! Yea!"

Almost too soon the bleachers had emptied and I found myself helping my brothers dismantle the refreshment stand. Around us milled a few stray ball players, my family, the BSC members . . . and Bart.

I was afraid to look at him. My team had beaten his. Was he mad at me all over again, but for a different reason? We have always known how competitive we are. Now, I wondered, could we *really* coach opposing teams and go out together, too? Let alone — maybe — be boy- and girlfriend?

I put off finding out by running to my friends and telling them what Cokie had done. They were all properly incensed.

"*Cokie* wrote the notes?" exclaimed Claudia.

"That — that sewer rat!" said Stacey, who still thinks in New York terms half the time.

"You should get back at her," said Jessi.

"I think I already did," I replied. "I told her I'd make sure that by Monday everyone at SMS and Bart's school will know what she's done. That's enough for Cokie. Besides, I don't want to continue this war with her."

Slowly my friends began to leave then, until only Shannon remained.

"Anything wrong?" she asked me.

"I don't know. I have a feeling Bart's upset. Do you think I should have let the Bashers win? I could have done that, you know."

"No way!" exclaimed Shannon.

"But will he still want to come to the Halloween Hop with me?"

"Go find out," said Shannon.

Reluctantly, I walked across the field to Bart, who was tossing equipment into a canvas bag.

"Hi," I said.

Bart glanced up. "Hey!" He grinned. "Good game."

I paused. He didn't sound mad. "So. Are you still up for the Hop?"

"Can't wait. Now tell me about the letters."

I did, after breathing a huge sigh of relief.

"Kristy!" called Charlie then.

"Bart!" called Mr. Taylor.

And then in unison they said, "Time to go!"

"See you Friday," whispered Bart, "but I'll probably talk to you before then."

"You got it, Coach!"

Later that afternoon, when I was recovering from the game, Shannon surprised me by coming over unannounced. She walked into

122

my room, where I was lying on the bed.

"I'm dead," I told her.

"Too dead for some tips?"

"What kind of tips?"

"Oh, makeup, stuff like that."

"I don't wear makeup," I told her.

"Not even to dances?"

I rolled over. "Hmm. I'm not sure."

"You want to look good for Bart, don't you?"

"I just want to look like myself. And if I'm going to look good, I'll look good for me."

"Okay. So what about makeup? And what are you going to wear?"

"Wear? I don't know."

"You do own a dress, don't you?"

"Of course I do . . . I think." I got up and went to my closet. "There must be a couple here somewhere." I pawed through my collection of shirts and sweaters. "Oh, here's one. I wore it when Mary Anne 's dad and Dawn's mom got married. And here's another. This is the one I wore when my mother and Watson got married." I held it up.

"Well, you can't wear that one to the dance," said Shannon. "It's much too dressy. It's a *long* dress for heaven's sake. Let me see the other one."

I put the fancy dress away and showed

Shannon the more casual one. "Of course, Bart and I could go in costume," I pointed out. "A lot of kids do go to the Hop in costume."

"But don't you want to look special for Bart?" asked Shannon. "And that dress is perfect. Who helped you pick it out?"

"Stacey did," I admitted.

"Well, it's great for a dance. Okay, put it on."

"How come?"

"Because I can't figure out your makeup and nail polish until I see you in the dress."

"*Nail* polish? No way! I'll wear makeup — a *little* makeup — but no nail polish."

"Okay, okay. Calm down."

Luckily, before we had gotten too far into the makeup ordeal, Watson stuck his head in my room and told me that Bart was on the phone.

"Thanks," I said, but as soon as he had left I moaned to Shannon, "I just know he's decided he doesn't want to go to the dance after all. I should have let the Bashers win the game today."

"*Kristy*," said Shannon sharply, "you should not have. Go see what Bart really wants. I'm sure he's not backing out."

I picked up the phone as if it were a dead

snake. I barely touched it. "Hello?" I squeaked. "Bart?"

"Hi, Coach," said Bart cheerfully. "Listen, you won't believe this. I have the greatest costumes for us to wear to the dance. I know we didn't say anything about costumes, but I was just up in our attic and I found — I *know* you're not going to believe this — but I found two *lobster* costumes. My parents wore them to a party once. A long time ago. I think my mom's costume would fit you. Do you want to wear it?"

Did I want to wear it? Of course I did! Then I wouldn't have to wear a dress. Or nail polish. "Oh, yes!" I cried. "Definitely. That's terrific, Bart. You know, they're giving out prizes for costumes this year. Scariest, funniest, that sort of thing. Hey, do these costumes have masks?"

"No," replied Bart. "We'll have to do a little makeup. Is that okay?"

"It's great!" I said. "Thanks. I'll talk to you soon. 'Bye!" I hung up and ran back to my room. "Shannon," I said, "that was Bart. Guess what. I'm going to do my own makeup. Watch this." I smeared my entire face with liquid rouge. I looked as red as a you-know-what.

Shannon gaped. "Kristy!! That's not a makeup job."

"It is when you're going to be a lobster."

I explained to Shannon about the costumes. Then I gleefully took off my dress and put it back in the closet.

"Kristy?" said Shannon.

"What?"

"You're weird."

"Thank you."

Shannon grinned at me. "You and Bart are going to have a great time," she said.

"I hope so," I replied.

CHAPTER 14

It was Friday night, the night of the Hallow-een Hop.

I stood in front of the full-length mirror in the bathroom.

I was wearing a lobster costume.

"Not bad," I murmured. I certainly did look like a lobster — if lobsters were able to stand up and walk on their tails with their legs waving around in front of them. I had antennae, the proper number of legs, and even claws. (The claws fitted over my hands, like mittens.) The other six legs were stiff with wire and were fastened to the body of the costume.

I was just applying the last of the rouge to my face when, "Aughhh!"

"Aughhh!" I shrieked back.

Karen was standing behind me. My costume had scared her, and she had scared me. "Is *that* what you're wearing to the dance to-night?" she asked, incredulous. "I thought when girls went to dances they wore beautiful gowns and ribbons or maybe pearls in their hair. And jewelry, lots of jewelry."

Karen moved beside me and gazed in the mirror. I'm sure she was picturing herself at a "big girl" dance, jewel bedecked and gorgeous.

"No, silly," I said, fluffing her hair. "I mean, usually people do get dressed up for a dance, but this is a Halloween dance, so Bart and I are wearing costumes. How do I look as a lobster?"

"Fine. Is Bart your boyfriend?"

"Maybe." I answered. "I'm not sure."

"How come you're not sure?"

"I'm just not, that's all." Usually, I like having Karen and Andrew live with us every other weekend, but sometimes Karen asks too many questions. So I asked her one instead, hoping she'd forget about Bart. "Is *your* Halloween costume ready?"

"Yup." (Karen, Andrew, David Michael, Emily, and a bunch of their friends were going to go trick-or-treating the next day as characters from *The Wizard of Oz*. Mom had hired me to take them around the neighborhood.)

"Well, I guess I'm as ready as I'll ever be," I told Karen.

"Are you nervous, Kristy?"

"A little." Actually, I was very nervous, but not for any reason Karen could imagine. Here are the reasons I was worried:

1. I'm not a great dancer, and it was hard enough to *walk* in my costume, let alone dance in it.

2. This was basically my first true date. I'd gone to dances before, but only with dweebs like Alan Gray, so those didn't count. And Bart and I had gone to the movies and stuff before, but usually on the spur of the moment, and definitely only as friends. I had a feeling tonight would be different.

3. Nobody at SMS, except my friends (and some enemies, who shall remain nameless) had seen Bart. Kids didn't bring dates from other schools very often, so Bart and I would have stood out as a couple even if we weren't dressed like lobsters. I was afraid that some kids might give Bart a hard time.

"Kristy!" called Watson from the front hall. "Are you ready to go? We told Bart we'd pick him up in ten minutes."

"Coming!" I called back. "Are you sure I look okay?" I asked Karen.

"Okay for a lobster," she replied.

I grinned. Then I gave her a good-night kiss. "See you in the morning."

"You're going to be out that late?"

"Pretty late. Oh, and guess who will be here when you wake up tomorrow?"

"Who?"

"Shannon, and Mary Anne, and all my friends from the Baby-sitters Club. We're going to have a sleepover after the dance."

"Goody!" said Karen.

"Kristy!" Watson called again.

"Okay, coming!" I ran downstairs. Watson drove me to Bart's house, we picked up the second lobster, and before I knew it, Watson was letting us off in front of SMS.

"Charlie and I will pick up you and your friends at ten-thirty, okay?" said Watson, as Bart and I struggled out of the car.

"Okay," I replied. "And thanks."

The Halloween Hop was a dance for all grades at SMS. Mary Anne and Logan were going to be there. Claudia was ecstatic because Woody Jefferson had asked her to go. Stacey had gotten up the nerve to invite Kelsey Bauman (the new boy she liked). Dawn and Jessi were going stag. And Mallory was going with Ben Hobart!

"Well," I said nervously to Bart as we entered my school, "this is SMS."

"It's *big*," said Bart. "I mean, it's not like I've never driven by it, but when you're this close up, it seems so much bigger than Stoneybrook Day School." Bart looked sort of nervous himself.

"Come on," I said, taking his claw, which was difficult to do.

I led Bart inside. We were entering the back way, near the gym, where the dance would be held. The BSC members (with or without dates) had agreed to meet there. I was relieved to find Stacey and Kelsey, Dawn, and Mary Anne and Logan already there. As soon as the others arrived, we entered the gym in a big bunch.

Right away, people began staring at Bart and me.

"Everyone's looking at us," I whispered to Mary Anne.

"It's just your costumes," she whispered back. "They're so unusual. Don't worry. No one's laughing."

But Bart and I gripped claws even more tightly.

"Come on," said Bart. "Let's get some punch."

So we did. After we had stood around for awhile, and people had gotten used to us, Bart said, "Do you want to dance? This band is *good*."

"Hey!" I exclaimed, as we headed for the dance floor, "maybe someday *your* band could play here. We're always looking for bands."

"Maybe," replied Bart, sounding excited at the prospect.

And so we began to dance. I soon realized that Bart couldn't tell if I was a good dancer or a rotten one. *Neither* of us could dance well with all the legs and claws and tentacles.

I relaxed and looked around the gym. It was decorated with black and orange streamers and balloons. And the chaperones (our teachers) were all in costumes! Bart and I whirled by Mary Anne and Logan, who were dressed as a witch and Frankenstein. We danced by Stacey and Kelsey, who were just dressed up. (Karen would have approved.) We passed by Dawn, dressed as Alice in Wonderland, who was dancing with a hunchback. (I didn't recognize him.)

And then we danced by Cokie Gray and Austin Bentley.

I prepared myself for remarks, but Cokie pretended not to notice Bart and me — even though I *know* she saw us. Good. Maybe our war was over. I didn't mind being ignored by Cokie. Anyway, a lot of kids at school were mad at her for sending the notes. I felt satisfied.

Bart and I took a break after awhile, had some more punch, and then returned to the dance floor. The first slow dance began. Yikes! A *slow* dance. Bart put his arms around my neck and we swayed back and forth, back and forth, in time to the music. Somehow, though, I had a feeling that I wasn't getting the full effect of things, what with those layers of foam between us. It didn't matter, though. A slow dance felt pretty nice.

When the band stopped for a break of their own, one of the teachers (Ms. Mandel, who was dressed as Snow White), stepped up to a microphone. "While the members of the band are taking a rest," she began, "I would like to present the prizes for the best costumes."

Bart and I glanced at each other, hopeful.

"Scariest costume prizes," said Ms. Mandel, "go to Danny Olssen and Tara Valentine, our space monsters. Funniest costume prizes go to Danielle Pitchard and Marcus Brown, the surfing dinosaurs. The prizes for the most unusual costumes go to our lobsters, Kristy Thomas and . . ."

I didn't even hear the rest of what Ms. Mandel had to say. "We won!" I exclaimed to Bart. "I wonder *what* we won." And then I added, "You don't think most unusual really means strangest, do you?"

"No," Bart assured me. "Besides, who cares? We won a coupon for a free large pizza at Pizza Express."

"You're kidding!"

"Nope. That teacher just announced it. Come on. We're supposed to go and collect our prize."

So Bart and I joined the other winners, who were surrounding Ms. Mandel. As our pizza coupons were handed out, everyone clapped.

Then the band members returned and the dancing began again. Bart and I danced until Bart looked at the clock on the wall and said, "Kristy, it's ten-fifteen. We better find your friends and get going."

"Oh," I said in disappointment, but I knew he was right. "Let's just finish this dance first, though." (It was a slow dance.)

So we did. And when the music ended, Bart leaned toward me and kissed me very gently on the cheek.

Ooh, I thought. So this is what it's like to be in love.

CHAPTER 15

"All right, I want to know *every*thing," said Shannon.

She and I, and Jessi, Stacey, Mary Anne, Mallory, Dawn, and Claudia were sitting around my bedroom. The dance was over. Scattered about the room were pieces of our costumes — Dawn's Alice in Wonderland dress, Mal's clown feet (she'd had a lot of trouble dancing at the Hop, and had had to take the shoes off and dance barefoot) Mary Anne's witch hat, and my lobster suit. The suit was huge and was standing in a corner, the tentacles waving ever so slightly.

My friends and I had all changed into our nightgowns. Shannon, Stacey, and I were lying on my bed on our stomachs with our feet in the air. Mallory, Dawn, Mary Anne, and Jessi were propped up in various places on the floor of my room. Dawn, in fact, was leaning against the bed, and Shannon was braiding her hair from above. Claudia was sitting at my desk, painting her nails.

"Why are you painting your nails *now?*" I asked her, looking at my watch.

"So I won't have to do it tomorrow," she replied simply.

"Come on, I want to hear about the dance," said Shannon again.

"All right," said Jessi. "I'll start. The gym was beautifully decorated. There were streamers and balloons everywhere — "

"Not that kind of stuff!" Shannon interrupted her. "The good stuff."

"The good stuff?" repeated Jessi. She and Mallory hadn't been to too many dances. They weren't sure what sort of information Shannon wanted.

"How about this?" said Stacey. "Cokie Gray was all dressed up. I mean, not in a costume, just really *dressed up*. She was wearing a lot of makeup, too, including false eyelashes." (I began to laugh. I knew what Stacey was going to say. I'd seen what had happened.) "And she leaned over the punch bowl and one of her lashes fell off and landed right in the punch."

"And Miranda Shillaber was standing there and she made the teacher who was in charge of the refreshments get a fresh bowl of punch because she said the first bowl had been contaminated by the eyelashes. I thought Cokie was going to kill her. She gave her a Look," I finished.

Shannon laughed. "So what else? Did you all dance?"

"Yup," answered Dawn. "No wallflowers here."

"Ben is a great dancer," said Mal dreamily.

"I danced with about eight different boys and they were all clods," announced Jessi, with disgust.

"That's because you're used to dancing with boys who take ballet," said Mal. "They're graceful."

"No, Jessi's right. Sixth-grade boys are clods," said Shannon knowingly. "Trust me. I remember. Half of them are all gangly, kind of like spiders, and the other half are so short you can hardly see them."

"When does it change?" asked Jessi.

"It's slow. A — a sort of — What's the word?" said Claudia, without looking up from her nail polish pursuits.

"A metamorphosis?" suggested Mary Anne.

"Yeah, that's it. A metamorphosis," said Claud. She held out one hand, examining her fingertips critically. "Not bad," she murmured. "Some day I'm going to go to the nail salon and get a French manicure."

I was about to ask what that was when Shannon said, "Come on. More details! More details! I can't stand not knowing what happened."

"Kristy and Bart won the prize for the most unusual costumes," said Dawn. She reached up to pat her head and see how the braiding was coming.

"Great," said Shannon. "What'd you win?"

"A coupon for a FREE LARGE pizza with everything," I answered.

"Ew," said Jessi. "Even anchovies?"

"Bart and I happen to like anchovies," I replied. "We have a lot in common."

"*Yeah*," said Stacey slyly.

Shannon peered across Stacey's back and over at me. "What does she mean?" she asked with interest.

"I — I — " (I couldn't get the words out.)

"Bart *kissed* her!" exclaimed Mal, unable to contain herself. "He kissed her at the dance right in front of everyone!"

"He kissed you?" cried Shannon. She dropped the braid she was working on. "*How* did he kiss you?"

"It was just a kiss on the cheek," I said. "And how did you know about that, Mal?" I asked.

Mary Anne giggled. "We all know," she said. "Everybody saw. He kissed you in the middle of the gym."

I tried to be embarrassed, but I don't think I even worked up a red face. I was sort of proud that my friends had seen Bart kiss me.

Mary Anne began to giggle.

"What?" I said.

"Bart is better than Alan Gray with M&M's in his eyes, isn't he?" she said.

We all laughed, except for Shannon, who didn't understand the true extent of Alan's pestiness.

"Alan," I began explaining to Shannon, "will do anything for attention. Once we gave Mary Anne a party" (I said that part quickly because Mary Anne had hated the party; we should have known better than to surprise her) "and Alan walked around with yellow M&M's squinted between his eyes, telling everyone he was Little Orphan Annie."

"I can assure you," said Shannon, "that Bart will never do that. At least not in public." She returned to Dawn's hair.

"Kristy?" Jessi spoke up softly. "Are you in love?"

I hesitated, knowing that by hesitating I was giving myself away. If any of my brothers had been in the room they would have teased me for about a year. But my friends wouldn't do that. They all just glanced at me and let the subject drop.

"Well," said Dawn, "tomorrow's Halloween."

"No . . . it's today," said Mal in a low voice, looking at her watch. "The time is twelve-oh-three."

"I'm taking Karen, Andrew, David Michael, Emily, and some of their friends trick-or-treating tomorrow," I said. "They're going to dress up as characters from *The Wizard of Oz*." I hoped I'd be able to keep my mind on the task. At the moment, all I could think of was Bart's kiss.

"That's cute," said Shannon. "Going as characters from *The Wizard of Oz*. They must be really excited."

"Half scared, too, I think. Remember how scary we used to think Halloween was?" I asked everyone.

"Definitely," said Mal. "I thought ghosts and vampires and things really did come out on Halloween night. The year I was six, I wouldn't even go trick-or-treating because I was afraid I wouldn't be able to tell the real spooks from the kids in costume."

"We were all pretty scared just last Halloween," pointed out Mary Anne. "Thanks to

Cokie and Grace and their friends."

"That's for sure," said Jessi.

"I'm kind of sorry I missed all that," said Stacey.

"No, you're not," Claud told her. "It was *really* scary."

"I'm glad Cokie gave herself away at the game last weekend," I said. "Can you imagine how we'd feel right now if I were still getting those notes?"

And at that very moment, a scream ripped through the air. I froze. Then I thawed out and looked at my friends. They were all looking at each other. None of *us* had screamed.

"Yikes!" I said. I tiptoed into the hallway — just in time to hear another scream. It came from Karen's room.

The door to Mom and Watson's bedroom opened then, and Watson rushed out. "Don't worry," he told me. "I think Karen's having a nightmare."

With a sigh, I returned to my friends. "Just Karen," I said. "Bad dream. Watson's taking care of her."

We began to get ready to go to sleep. We put away our nail polish and barrettes, shoved our junk into a corner of the room, and my friends rolled out their sleeping bags. I was going to sleep in my bed. Even so, seven sleeping bags made the floor of the room pretty crowded.

Scritch, scratch. Scritch, scratch.

Mary Anne jumped a mile. "What was that?"

"Just branches scraping my windows," I said carelessly. I wasn't going to let Halloween spook *me*. "A storm must be blowing in."

I waited until everyone was settled in their sleeping bags. Then I pulled back the covers on my bed and found . . . a kidnapping note on my pillow. It was all I could do not to shriek, but I didn't want Watson to come dashing into my room. Instead I just gasped.

"What? What's wrong?" asked Dawn.

"This is," I whispered. I held up the note. It was made of letters cut from magazines and newspapers and said, "I am coming for you tonight. I will be there at 3:00 A.M. There's no way to escape me."

Everyone crawled out of their sleeping bags and was reading the note wide-eyed, looking ready to scream.

Everyone except Shannon. She began to laugh.

"*Shannon!* Did you do this?" I demanded.

Shannon couldn't control herself. "Yes," she said, giggling. "I didn't know what to do with myself all evening while I waited for you guys to come back from the dance. So I made that letter. It took hours."

"I'll treasure it always," I said sarcastically.

"You aren't mad, are you, Kristy?" asked Shannon.

"Nah. In fact, you just gave me an idea."

"What, I'm afraid to ask," said Mary Anne.

"Come on. I'll show you."

If any of us had been sleepy before, we weren't now. Shannon's note had given us a second wind. So everyone jumped up and followed me out of my room, down the hall, down the stairs, and into the den, where our computer is set up. I slipped a disk into the drive and typed out:

My dearest, darling Cokie,
    You are the light of my life. You make the sun rise every morning. You make the flowers grow, yellow-dappled and dewy. Every day I watch you. I watch you in the halls and the cafeteria and science class. You are a creature more gorgeous than a goddess. Please accept this heartfelt invitation to dissect a frog with me.

                    Always and forever,
                    Your Mystery Perspirer

Everyone was howling, and Shannon asked, "What are you going to do with that note, Kristy?"

"Stick it in Cokie's locker on Monday morning."

"Don't you think she's going to know who wrote it?"

"Yes," I replied, "and I don't care. I know I said I didn't want to continue the war with Cokie, but I can't help it. This is too good an idea to pass up. Come on, you guys. Let's go to bed."

And so, note in hand, I led my friends back to my room, where we promptly fell asleep and didn't wake up until eleven o'clock the next morning.

About the Author

ANN M. MARTIN did *a lot* of baby-sitting when she was growing up in Princeton, New Jersey. Now her favorite baby-sitting charge is her cat, Mouse, who lives with her in her Manhattan apartment.

Ann Martin's Apple Paperbacks include *Yours Turly, Shirley; Ten Kids, No Pets; With You and Without You; Bummer Summer;* and all the other books in the Baby-sitters Club series.

She is a former editor of books for children, and was graduated from Smith College. She likes ice cream, the beach, and *I Love Lucy;* and she hates to cook.

Look for #39

POOR MALLORY

I entered our house through the garage door. The rec room was silent and empty. So I ran upstairs to the living room. Everyone was sitting there, either on the couch or chairs, or on the floor.

No one had to tell me what the news was. I could see for myself.

"Oh, Dad," I said, letting out a breath. "I'm sorry," said Dad simply.

"Hey, you don't have to apologize," I told him quickly. "It wasn't your fault."

"He got a pink slip," Claire spoke up. She was sitting on the floor, playing with Vanessa's hair. "He got it at five o'clock."

"Those stinkers!" I exploded. "Why did they wait so long to tell you you were fired? Why didn't they give out all the slips in the morning, instead of driving people crazy making them wait all day?"

"I don't know." Dad sighed. "Maybe they

146

were still making decisions about who should go and who should stay."

"Well, I still think the people who run your company are really stale."

"Look," said Dad, sounding cross, "I got fired and that's that."

"*Okay. Sorry*," I replied. I was taken aback. Dad usually doesn't talk that way. He's a sensitive, gentle person.

"Come on," said Mom. "Let's have dinner."

"Is it okay to eat? Shouldn't we be saving our food for when we really need it?" asked Nicky. He wasn't being sassy. He *meant* it.

"For pity's sake, we aren't destitute," answered Dad.

"What's 'dessatoot'?" Claire whispered to me as we followed Mom and Dad into the kitchen. I felt bad for her. I knew she was whispering because she didn't want Dad to hear her and get mad at *her*.

"Destitute," I corrected her, "and it means as poor as you can get."

"Very, *very* poor?" whispered Claire.

"Right. Very, very poor. And we aren't very, very poor," (yet, I thought) "so don't worry, okay?"

"Okay."

Read all the books
in the Baby-sitters Club series
by Ann M. Martin

149

titles continued...

☐	MG42501-3	#28	Welcome Back, Stacey!	$2.95
☐	MG42500-5	#29	Mallory and the Mystery Diary	$2.95
☐	MG42498-X	#30	Mary Anne and the Great Romance	$2.95
☐	MG42497-1	#31	Dawn's Wicked Stepsister	$2.95
☐	MG42496-3	#32	Kristy and the Secret of Susan	$2.95
☐	MG42495-5	#33	Claudia and the Great Search	$2.95
☐	MG42494-7	#34	Mary Anne and Too Many Boys	$2.95
☐	MG42508-0	#35	Stacey and the Mystery of Stoneybrook	$2.95
☐	MG43565-5	#36	Jessi's Baby-sitter	$2.95
☐	MG43566-3	#37	Dawn and the Older Boy	$2.95
☐	MG43567-1	#38	Kristy's Mystery Admirer	$2.95
☐	MG41588-3		Baby-sitters on Board! Super Special #1	$2.95
☐	MG42419-X		Baby-sitters' Summer Vacation Super Special #2	$2.95
☐	MG42499-8		Baby-sitters' Winter Vacation Super Special #3	$3.50
☐	MG42493-9		Baby-sitters' Island Adventure Super Special #4	$3.50
☐	MG43745-3		The Baby-sitters Club 1990-91 Student Planner and Date Book	$7.95
☐	MG43744-5		The Baby-sitters Club 1991 Calendar	$8.95
☐	MG43803-4		The Baby-sitters Club Notebook	$1.95

Available wherever you buy books...or use this order form.

Scholastic Inc., P.O. Box 7502, 2931 E. McCarty Street, Jefferson City, MO 65102

Please send me the books I have checked above. I am enclosing $_____
(please add $2.00 to cover shipping and handling). Send check or money order — no cash or C.O.D.s please.

Name _____

Address _____

City _____ State/Zip _____

Please allow four to six weeks for delivery. Offer good in the U.S. only. Sorry, mail orders are not available to residents of Canada. Prices subject to change.

BSC390

WIN A TRIP TO NEW YORK CITY!

Enter **THE BABY-SITTERS CLUB®** *Adventure Giveaway*

"Where are the Baby-sitters going on their next Super Special Adventure?"

Guess the right place and win the trip of your dreams! We'll send the Grand Prize Winner of this Giveaway and his/her parent or guardian on an all-expense paid weekend (2 nights, 3 days) to New York City! Just fill in the coupon below and return by November 30, 1990.

500 Second Prize Winners get Baby-sitters Club Sun Visors!

Hint:
The Baby-sitters will need their sun visors on their next Super Special adventure!

Rules: Entries must be postmarked by November 30, 1990. Winners will be picked at random and notified by mail. No purchase necessary. Valid only in the U.S. Void where prohibited. Taxes on prizes are the responsibility of the winners and their immediate families. Employees of Scholastic Inc.; its agencies, affiliates, subsidiaries; and their immediate families not eligible. For a complete list of winners, send a self-addressed stamped envelope to The Baby-sitters Club Adventure Giveaway, Giveaway Winners List, at the address provided below.

Fill in the coupon below or write the information on a 3" x 5" piece of paper and mail to: **THE BABY-SITTERS CLUB ADVENTURE GIVEAWAY**, Scholastic Inc., P.O. Box 7500, Jefferson City, MO 65102.

The Baby-sitters Club Adventure Giveaway

The Baby-sitters' next Super Special Adventure will be in: _____

_____

Name_____ Age_____

Street_____

City_____ State_____ Zip_____

Where did you buy this *Baby-sitters Club* book?

❏ Bookstore   ❏ Drugstore   ❏ Supermarket   ❏ Library

❏ Book Club   ❏ Book Fair   ❏ Other_____(specify)   BSC190